This collection of sixty-three stories is as rich and varied as a patisserie, as nasty and brutish as a Japanese architect in the mid-sixties, as delicate as the swift-moving scents in the coastal air at midnight. To call these stories short-shorts or "flash fiction" is to do them a disservice. While some are indeed short, and many are pleasantly flashy, every one hits home with the weight of boxer's punch, every one is more beautiful, and more fun, than the last. This is a first rate performance by an artist to be reckoned with.

FREDERICK BARTHELME, AUTHOR OF
THERE MUST BE SOME MISTAKE

Like Donald Barthelme, Damian Dressick finds himself on the leading edge of the junk phenomena. The thingness of things falls apart delightfully right before our dilated eyes. Fun for the whole goddamn nuclear family.

MICHAEL MARTONE, AUTHOR
OF *MICHAEL MARTONE*

Fables of the Deconstruction is funny, sad, dreamy, and brutal. The stories here veer off in strange directions, happily disobedient to the conventions that plague so much of our current grindingly cautious literature. This is a credit to Damian Dressick, an excitable and exciting new writer who will probably be a big deal someday and, in fact, if you check your heart, already is.

STEVE ALMOND, AUTHOR OF *ROCK AND ROLL WILL SAVE YOUR LIFE*

Damian Dressick writes with gusto and sly humor, and *Fables of the Deconstruction* introduces a bold and robust new voice of impressive range. A heady debut.

GARIELLE LUTZ, AUTHOR OF *WORSTED*

Damian Dressick's *Fables of the Deconstruction* expertly explores the question: *why not?* Wandering through Dressick's terrain, you can leave your own (real) life behind for a while. Sit back and enjoy. This little book will make you both happy and sad—with footnotes.

SHERRIE FLICK AUTHOR OF *I CALL THIS FLIRTING* AND *RECONSIDERING HAPPINESS*

In *Fables of the Deconstruction*, a long-awaited debut collection, Damian Dressick enchants with a smorgasbord of tragic, strange, beautiful, and darkly funny stories. The author's range and variety of tone set this stunning debut collection apart from any other single-author collection of recent memory. Each piece works like a straight shot of espresso for the spirit, simultaneously sobering and mysterious. Dressick's tales are profound, heartbreaking and addictively fun to read.

MEG POKRASS, AUTHOR OF *THE DOG LOOKS HAPPY UPSIDE DOWN* AND CO-EDITOR OF *BEST MICROFICTION*

FABLES OF THE DECONSTRUCTION

DAMIAN DRESSICK

CLASH

CONTENTS

FABLES OF THE DECONSTRUCTION

IF I COULD ONLY TELL YOU ONE STORY

Parts I and II
—for Jan Beatty

part I

IF I COULD ONLY TELL you one story, it would be this:

One crisp fall afternoon near the beginning of October when the autumn leaves shone like a bouquet of golden chalices lit through roseglass cathedral windows, my mother did a little dance—a jig or a reel perhaps—before launching herself from the observation deck of a mid-rise building in Albany, New York. Halfway between the blue screen of sky and the pavement, hard and black, she was transformed into a sleek bird, rapacious and perfect and never to be seen again.

part II

If I could only tell you one story and it had to be *true*—it would be this:

When I was fifteen years old my mother caught me stealing dishes from the mayor of Scranton, Pennsylvania. I had been helping out in the city hall kitchen where my mother worked as a maid. When she caught me, shirt bulging with salad plates and trousers pockets lined with teacups, she scowled before she smiled and said: "The silver. My precious, precious idiot. Take the silver."

THE FOOD SPEAKERS

IN OLD ITALY, long ago, nestled far up in the mountains, where the thin air chilled and the pure sun shone, was a village that for generations had dispensed with language in favor of food as the agreed method of communication.

Crisp pastries plumped with Seek No More apples smoothed the way in courtship. Demitasses of steaming espresso suggested a need to be vigilant. Tureens of cold parsnip soup seasoned with bitter herbs alerted a man to his wife's budding anger.

Neither Bibles nor portraits, but recipes were passed down through families. What better way, the villagers thought, to tell a girl her great-grandmother had been hot- tempered and adventurous than serving her a stew so spiced with cayenne and paprika it singed the tongue just to taste it? Or to let children know Uncle Gio came from Naples than placing before them heaps of fusilli doused with a red sauce stewed from dozens of the season's finest heirloom tomatoes and bursting with fresh basil?

Every year, at mid-winter's eve, when days were short and friendships brittle, the village pulled itself together for a tremendous feast. Ham coated with honey and platters of trout and heaps of succulent greens graced a table the length of a horse-barn and all the villagers sat down together to break bread and mend fences. The meaning of this meal for the villagers was, "We are a good people of hearty stock, living close to the earth. Our hearts know the bitter and the sweet, and like meat cured in the smokehouse, we will last."

Year after year, the festival meal became more and more elaborate. It started with men chancing the high, snowy passes to trek to the rail station at Abruzzi to bring back fresh lamb from Rome. Then, boys borrowed bicycles, and later cars, to retrieve seasonal fruits from the Sun Coast in Spain.

As this augmentation increased, the meaning of the festival evolved to signify, "We are a prosperous village, industrious and willing to exert every effort to get our due."

By the time fresh shrimp and oysters were being trucked in from the islands far to the south, the festival had come to mean, "As the best and most eloquent village in all Italy, *la Alimentare Gli Altoparlanti*, or the Food Speakers, we are entitled to know every dish on the green earth and every delicacy plucked from the deep blue sea." Nearly all of the people in the village were proud of its growing fluency and myriad flutes of champagne were hoisted high in celebration.

The first year the lobsters packed in ice were flown in by helicopter, an old man rose to castigate his fellow villagers for forsaking the time-honored ways of their ancestors. His fork trembling, he fed everyone seated around the long table a small bite of each of the old, traditional dishes and flung, in turn, each platter of the arriviste foods to the snowy ground. As he did this, all the villagers raised their bitter cups of espresso at once to signal agreement and lock-in-step placed them carefully back in their saucers without having drunk to show penitence.

But as the meal ended, they brought the old man a small plate of almonds sprinkled with a fine dusting of poison. In the old language of food, this meant, "Shut the hell up, you old fossil. You've talked enough."

With no protest, the old man lodged himself quietly in a chair at the end of the long festival table and sitting alone ate the almonds, chewing meticulously, happy—at least for this last, short day—to have put things right.

FOUR HARD FACTS ABOUT WATER

1. Mixed with Dewar's White Label whiskey and served in a highball glass with shaved ice, it will cost nearly eleven dollars, on average, in most bars within two blocks of New York City's Houston Street.

2. Many Christians believe a thorough dousing in concert with a contrite heart represents a first, but critically important, step on the road to the development and maintenance of a personal relationship with Jesus Christ.

3. Breaststroke, backstroke, butterfly, Australian crawl, take your pick—as Pennsylvania's Junior State champion 1994, you go through it like a fish.

4. After your two-year-old daughter trips and falls unseen into the neighbor's in- ground pool while you are in their summer house trying to find steak sauce, your involvement with Fact One can consume your life, costing you your spouse and job and nearly, if not quite all, your self-esteem. Fact Two will be rendered utterly powerless in the face of this tragedy and Fact

Three will come to be the way you define irony—when slurring to strangers who have already asked you once to please leave them alone as closing time approaches at O'Flanagan's, always a little quicker than you'd like.

THE FUNGIBLE TRAJECTORIES OF CAROL

IN HER LATE 30s and attractive, Carol uses sex.

Belonging to fifteen Internet dating apps and employing more than 25 screen names, she has been meeting for sex with as many as six different men—sometimes two before lunch—each day. Missionary, girl-on-top, doggie, Carol is ambivalent. She is motivated in this only by quantity and novelty of partner.

Carol's employment of sex serves, at this point, a broad array of purposes. Mood enhancement. Self-congratulation. Nourishment. Sustenance. Comfort. As a reason to punish herself. As the punishment. To add drama to what is an otherwise dull life. To feel desired. Needed. Loved.

As a freelance writer living in a major metropolitan area, Carol's schedule and surroundings not uncomfortably allow this kind of behavior. As a lapsing Catholic and someone who is reasonably concerned about the contraction of STDs, her ethics and health concerns do their best to rein it in.

As American readers plunged into this recounting in the opening decades of the 21st century, we will probably not be comfortable with this going on much longer. As Carol's "bad behavior" began approximately three months ago—on the heels of her breaking things off with her fiancé—we can likely abide this acting out only for a few more weeks, a month at most. So where do things go from here?

• If, at gun point, you would announce yourself a political liberal, try ending A:

• If, on the other hand, you consider yourself a political conservative, try ending B:

• If you have no distinct political beliefs, there are probably better uses to be made of your time than a careful reading of this story. Please skip to the end.

A. Following a pregnancy scare, Carol sees the error of her ways and sets up an appointment at the counseling center. After being diagnosed with hyper-sexual hypomania, Carol is prescribed a five milligram daily dose of a powerful mood stabilizer and spends several difficult months in therapy where she does her best to work out issues involving self-esteem, her relationship with her father and the meaning of interaction with men in general. After a fusillade of false "breakthroughs," Carol eventually comes to understand that her body chemistry predisposes her to react to stress by seeking out even greater stress. Terming this "Carol's Fucked Up Law of Relativity," she enrolls in an M.F.A. program well-respected for its competencies in creative non-fiction, where she writes and revises her bestselling memoir, "My Life As a Slut."

B. After a condom breaks while Carol engages in a threesome at the Holiday Inn, she contracts HIV. Due to her habits and lack of self-control, she spreads the disease to two more men before the results of her test come back from the free clinic at Planned Parenthood. Upon learning that she is responsible for the men's illnesses, Carol's guilt rules her life like an absolutist monarch. She becomes dangerously depressed and takes to blowing what little freelance money she is still capable of earning on binge drinking and crystal meth. Both of these substances dramatically reduce the effectiveness of the retroviral cocktail prescribed by her doctor, although this matters less than one would suspect, as Carol loses her health insurance six months down the road and can no longer afford the medicine. As her body thins dangerously, Carol maxes out her credit cards to finance a trip to Italy where she spends her last drifting days sniffing Afghani heroin and watching the sun retreat slowly into the slate blue Mediterranean.

In many stories of this length, it is customary to withhold a critical piece of information, a fact that makes you view the story in a wholly other light. Even though the multiple choice form employed in "The Fungible Trajectories of Carol" may have already come close to exhausting your readerly tolerance for innovation or gimmick, this tale is no exception.

Here is the end:

Carol (or her ravaged and angry ghost, depending) arrives at your flat. She may be holding a weapon, a machine pistol, perhaps, or simply clutching a cup of very hot tea, but what is non-negotiable is her demand you explain to her satisfaction—and the very best of your ability—your rationale for answering as you did and until you do there isn't even the slightest chance she's going anywhere.

CLEANLINESS

I COME HOME to the smell of meat. Not the subtle wafting of sirloin tips or pounded cutlets sautéing as a prelude to being served with thick sticks of asparagus, but the concentrated odor of raw meat—pungent, sweet, overpowering—as if our front door led to the killing room of an abattoir.

Briefcase still in hand, overcoat across my shoulders like a cape, I follow the broken trail of Styrofoam packaging and plastic wrap through our cramped shotgun apartment to the bathroom. Chops and shanks, roasts and ribs oxidize in a brown heap next to the space heater.

My boyfriend, a firefighter who's recovering from a bad time, hunches in our cramped tub drizzling the remains of one of the packages through his thinning hair. When I ask what has happened, he smiles beatifically up from the tub.

"I spent a hundred and seventy dollars at the butcher shop," he says.

He is nude. His pubic hair is soaked flat against his body. A pool of thin red fluid has formed beneath him and rises nearly to the tops of his pale feet. Although wildly inappropriate, this macabre spectacle reminds me of the time my little sister Carol got her period in the pool.

"I am being washed in the blood of the lamb," he tells me finally.

My boyfriend is relaxed. Unconcerned with my reaction, he keeps on, wringing what I believe to be a shoulder chop across his hairless chest a little below the nipples.

"That's a metaphor," I tell him. "That means if you go to church, God will forgive your sins."

"Are you so sure of that?"

And although in fifteen minutes I will call the psychiatrist and Louis will spend several days under observation before returning home with a Zyprexa prescription, for this one luminous moment, the way he looks up at me from his pool of watery redness, the *relief* etched across his face as with numinous acid, this man I love makes me wonder.

ACCRUAL

THE CARDINALS CAME FIRST. Their bright plumage a welcome splash of color in the late winter sunlight, my wife and I would gather at the kitchen window clutching our steaming mugs and watch them greedily at the feeder. We'd eye their conical beaks dipping into the bed of sunflower and canary seeds and bask in the pleasantness of their arrival. Like a visit from favored, distant relatives or the commencement of a long-awaited sporting event, their morning perching signaled a magic time, a joyful respite from the rigors and knocks of our overscheduled lives.

Then the orioles came. Their hunting-vest orange chests were less dazzling than the cardinals' spectacular plumage, but together the colors made for a nice contrast and at any rate we took great pleasure in listening to their high twitter and watching them dance and flutter between the branches of our dwarf cedars.

When the blue jays appeared, however, we were somewhat less thrilled. They were avaricious and bossy and perhaps it was this reflection of our own less palatable qualities that caused us to bear them so much ill-will. But they were colorful and spunky and eventually we came to appreciate the harsh music of their down-slurred trill.

It was the rattlesnake incursion that started us suspecting something uncanny and not entirely avian might be afoot. Not that the birds had stopped coming, even though the feeder was long depleted. In fact, dozens of them roosted cozily out of reach above the brood of newly arrived vipers lazing on the Rorschachs of pea gravel separating the hydrangea from the tiger lilies and bleeding hearts.

Our mornings, formerly cherished oases in task-choked days, were now consumed with dodging bird droppings or even errant diamondback strikes in acts simple and quotidian as retrieving the mail from its shiny silver box or sipping diluted pomegranate juice on the brick patio. Repeated calls to the city's various extermination outfits were met only by a motley assemblage of drunks trundling unsteadily up our sidewalk and onto the porch, where they tried loudly to interest us in quaffing schooners of their homebrewed beer.

Nearly overwhelmed—a carpet of diamondback rattlers stretching across our yard, over which perched an increasingly menacing flock of blue jays, cardinals and orioles that over the last week had swelled to Hitchcockian proportions, and the home brewing contingent having torn out the flowerbeds to make room for their crop of Bavarian hops and frittering away the remains of our cord wood firing the barley malting kiln they erected on the front porch—we imagined things couldn't get much worse.

Only when Luis, our postman, was chased up the block by a trio of bear cubs did we realize how wrong we were. Snarling almost joyfully, they treed the poor bastard in Wilson's white birch, taking turns batting at his Vibram-soled walking shoes each time he refreshed his iffy grip. Of course their growling was nothing compared to the terrifying roar that thundered from the gaping maws of the mated pair of tigers that days later ate the pizza delivery boy. Pausing in our fortification of the picture window with organic potting soil-stuffed sandbags, we looked on in horror as the big cats polished off him and his insulated delivery satchel without so much as a belch.

But it wasn't the marauding bands of apex predators that finally demanded we seek some insight into what was happening to our neighborhood, rather the sudden influx of Franciscan friars. Almost overnight, the business casual attired teachers at Woodbine Avenue Elementary were replaced by severe and befrocked Jesuits, terrifying our tiny, agnostic children and sending my wife and me out to risk life and limb to procure intel. Stealthily we crept from house to house, peering through windows, hiding behind Camrys and Accords, scouring the manicured lawns and neatly trimmed hedgerows for clues to the strange and increasingly infelicitous goings-on.

When, peeking through their draperied windows, we saw that many of our formerly flag-waving, almost disturbingly patriotic neighbors had begun to demonstrate pronounced communist leanings, centering polished marble mini-busts of Stalin on their mantles between the Hummels and ceramic urns and replacing Old Glory with the Hammer and Sickle, we began to formulate a theory.

The mass incursion of twins two days later confirmed what we'd formerly regarded as left-field suspicions. Taken together with the influx of cardinals, orioles, blue jays, diamondbacks, cubs, tigers, padres, brewers and reds, the sets of identical, tow-headed teens roaming our streets could mean only one thing: our neighborhood was being invaded by baseball mascots.

"It's not so much the Mariners' incipient shore leave that concerns me," Kelly offered as we cowered in the living room, occasionally peering over the window sash to reassure ourselves that the closest tiger was still engaged in devouring the entrails of a wayward twin. "But when the Pirates come, Damian, I think we're well and truly fucked."

She had an excellent point. Living in Pittsburgh, and truth be told at loose ends since the blue jays, how could we expect to hold off wave after wave of crazed, violent buccaneers questing for booty?

We scrambled those next fast-moving days. Doing our best not to end up as *amuse bouche* for the prowling tigers and marauding bears as they pitilessly stalked Woodbine Avenue, or be gunned down by an errant crossbow bolt as the padres set out to rid the neighborhood once and for all of the godless Reds, we strung our newly purchased razor-wire, buried our army-surplus anti-personnel mines and commenced with the digging of a small moat. Taking every conceivable measure to Pirate-proof our home, we even went so far as to load up the bird feeder with poison-parrot pellets.

Days later, however, when we discovered the Kandinsky's corner lot raised ranch mashed into splinters and in its place nothing but colossal footprints, we began to suspect that we had somehow miscalculated the rampaging mascots' order of arrival.

"Kelly," I asked. "Doesn't San Francisco have a baseball team?"

Later that night, as we practiced our parries and thrusts in preparation for the impending Pirate assault, the clatter of hooves and a fusillade of gunfire drew us to the window. Peering over the sandbags, we watched as one of the unfortunate becowled padres was ridden down by a quartet of self-righteous Texas lawmen. As the horsemen dismounted to string up their quarry, my wife informed me she'd had an inspiration.

"We've got to pit Ranger against Padre," my wife intoned conspiratorially. "Padre against Red."

At first I thought the stress of the situation had gotten the better of her and I'd have to watch my back as well as my front, but when I saw her laser printing dozens of copies of *The Communist Manifesto*, photocopying Rent-a-Rack catalogues from MailOrderInquisition.com and speed reading the middle chapters of *Gulliver's Travels*, I started to get the picture.

We started small, offering the Rangers flagons of beer as bounties on the snake skins and cub and tiger pelts. Then, with the ranks of cubs, diamondbacks and tigers thinned (and after we'd stored up enough beer to last the rest of the winter), we turned in the Brewers to the Liquor Control Board for commercial brewing without a license. Next, we schooled the Rangers in Lilliputian combat tactics and battle strategies, enabling a quick dispatch of one house-stomping Giant. From there, it was no great leap to incite a bloody and decimating anarchist riot, fatally setting the Reds against the Rangers.

The following week—employing a few choice 14th century quotes citing the evils of religious tolerance—we encouraged the Padres to convert the Reds by trials which must be described as unspeakably brutal. Suffice it to say, few survived.

It was only then we discovered that Pirates weren't coming—rumor had it they disbanded to join up with the Mariners. We later learned this was the only way they could envision being involved in a winning season in the foreseeable future.

"What about all these damn priests?" I asked my wife. "We can't live in a neighborhood ruled by Torquemada."

"Just you wait," she said.

And she was right. It took a few weeks of suffering enforced fish on Fridays and compulsory morning church attendance, but one bright Saturday in early April, the Angels came, from California or heaven, neither of us felt compelled to ask. But when they did, they drove the Padres from Woodbine Avenue like St. Patrick chasing the snakes from Ireland.

QUITTING WITH JIMMY

THREE DEEP IN line at the 7-Eleven off Route 46 in Hackettstown, New Jersey, our eyes are loosely fixed on a pimply clerk stymied by the spewing, renegade Slushie machine, when HE eases the gleaming Spyder into the parking lot.

At first we think he's a fake, an impostor striding across the macadam in his bright, too-tight jeans, lizard skin boots and T-shirt clinging to that muscled body like a second skin, but when he yanks open the safety glass door and enters in a penumbra of cinematic lighting—always backlit and shown to advantage—while we wilt, washed out under the humming fluorescents, the seeds of belief have been duly sown.

He nods to each of us in turn. Just the smallest curt adjustment of the chin, a miracle of understatement. Cocking his hip and jamming a grease-stained hand into his signature windbreaker with flawless casualness, he assumes his place at the register.

We coalesce around him. Gazes lowered, the women among us—and at least one of the men—fan their flushing faces with PennySavers and oversized Garden State Cash 4 Life lottery tickets, eyes glued to his high, perfectly formed butt cheeks.

His straight, bright teeth dazzle. His clear light eyes bewitch.

When he drawls, "Hey, uh, Slim, slide me a pack of them Camel cigarettes," it is poetry. It is sublime.

Rapt, we watch him fling the pack against the meat of his hand with a series of vigorous, but disaffected slaps. As the clerk backs away from the counter, refusing to take his proffered bill, our eyes light on his slim, white fingers as he fruitlessly pats himself down, searching for the tell-tale bulge of a Zippo.

In one swift motion, we collectively reach into our pockets, purses, jackets and fannypacks, seeking out the elusive match, lighter, flint and steel—anything—as he deftly yanks away the pack's cellophane tail and shakes a filterless white cylinder from the tiny rectangular cube of desert.

The amalgam of smile and sneer gracing his narrow, high-browed face as he leans into the nearest lit match nourishes our fragile outlaw souls like sunlight on winter wheat. The scent of burning tobacco mingling with his honest Indiana sweat takes us back to 1,000 unlived Midwest, teenage drive-in nights, when we were innocent and well-intentioned and the wide, wild world was our unsullied and flawless oyster.

"Excuse me, sir," the clerk says kiboshing our star struck, nicotine-infused reverie. "Sir, there's no smoking in the store."

"That so?" he asks, pulling the cigarette from his plump lips.

His pained grimace spreads from one of us to the next like a prairie fire. The lowered stick of tobacco smolders, penduluming at his trim waist as he attempts to discern if the clerk is somehow kidding.

When, in the long moments following the clerk's remarkably concise disquisition on the surgeon general's 1964 report on the hazardous effects of smoking and the subsequent hard fought court battles and ensuing legislation enacted to protect the public health, the 7-Eleven becomes remarkably quiet, he is the first to speak.

"Jesus wept," he says.

He relinquishes his grip on the burning cigarette and lets it drop to the floor. Like a ballerina performing a reluctant *tendu*, he raises the pointed toe of his high-polished Western boot and grinds a brown arc of tobacco flakes across the grimy terrazzo.

"That's it for me, kids," he tells us. "Not another butt. At 24, I am just too young to die."

On his way out, he shovel passes the Camel pack into a dented metallic waste can.

Watching his Spyder chirp a quick 180, roar onto the highway and shrink in the stripmall distance, we talk among ourselves in mumbles, our words clipped, our gestures shot through with unspeakable angst.

We want to warn him. We want to warn him about the H-Bomb and *Perestroika*, school shootings, the Internet and 9/11. Most urgently though, we want to warn him about a man with the unlikely name of Turnupseed and something horrible that's going to happen in the desert.

But if we can't save him, maybe the best we can do is save ourselves. Each in turn, we sidle toward the door and with a minor flourish ricochet our respective packs of coffin nails into the battered trash can as we exit the store back to our minivans and subcompacts, our steps imbued perhaps with just the smallest bit of newfound *joie de vivre* and borrowed swagger.

WE MUST LEAVE THIS ARID LAND
WHERE THE RELENTLESS SUN
BEATS DOWN

THE SOFT-SOLED bottoms of her feet inches above the rutted asphalt, Sabine floats down the loose, twisting curves of Laurel Canyon Boulevard. The sequined hem of her diaphanous dress trails behind her like the train of a wedding gown; she is soundless as a ghost.

Sabine is going to Fred Segal to drink a hazelnut latte in the sun and purchase several pairs of elegant, imported socks.

The socks are to be a present for her lover, a corrupt and on-the-lam portfolio manager who is, unbeknownst to Sabine, presently shacked up in a mid-priced hotel in Palm Desert with a 22 year-old production assistant. The assistant's name is also Sabine and she has recently come off a nine-week assignment getting coffee and being berated by a prominent director whose heartfelt film is a favorite for this year's Academy Award®.

Disturbingly clear, the day is one of the few each year that the small island next to Santa Catalina can be easily seen from the narrow, cantilevered deck that juts out from Sabine's bedroom.

With uncharacteristic industry, Sabine's two thick-bodied Labrador retrievers have dragged a pair of Eames chairs from their proper place in front of the fireplace out onto the narrow deck. Their tails tucked genteelly under their hindquarters, they sip Darjeeling tea from tiny, fragile cups and watch the sun strike the Pacific Ocean in the distance.

"Woof," says Luciano, the wiser and more resigned of the two.

"You can say that again," says the other.

Finishing their tea to the dregs, the dogs plot how they will distract Sabine in order to facilitate an opportunity to shred, rip and eventually eat the newly-purchased socks of the unscrupulous portfolio manager when he returns from the mid-priced hotel in the desert.

Where does a story go from a place like this? Talking dogs? Floating women? A clear day in Los Angeles? If we look to the title for direction, it suggests that someone must leave a hot, dry place that is doing them no good. The portfolio manager shacked up in Palm Desert—he certainly qualifies. So then, does the production assistant. But alas, both seem far too minor characters to be referenced in the title.

Maybe the hot, dry place is Laurel Canyon and the dogs are the ones who must leave—search out a better life in which they are cared for by a thoughtful, nurturing master, one who is not so completely consumed by her attempt to win an Academy Award® with her heartfelt, yet overly-determined film, that she goes through life entirely unaware of how remarkable they have become, learning Italian on the sly so as to belt out arias from Verdi's *Aida* next to the grand piano in the great room when she is away on location.

Then again, maybe the story is some type of meta-fiction and it is you or me that must leave this California, this lotus land of surfers and jasmine. But no, that can't be right. I have no idea where you are reading this. And I have not lived in Laurel

Canyon for years and anyway I am writing this from a coffee shop in Union Square in New York where it's pissing down rain.

The truth must be just as you suspected all along. It's high time for Sabine herself to take it on the hoof. Yes. She just needs a little push. A bit of encouragement. An assurance that she deserves and is capable of better. That would surely make for a story with much more depth than one in which the main appeal is the conceit of talking animals.

Sabine, inside you is a hot, dry place where the rain never falls and the sun is assiduous as judgment. If you are listening, you must move on.[1] Do you hear me? Move on. The California inside you is sterile as Mars.

---

1. Of course, if your name is not Sabine, but you find your own interior landscape similarly barren, then by all means, you should move on too.

ANOTHER NIGHT WITH JIM

TONIGHT, you're working again with Jim and that's something about which it's hard to be happy. It's not so much his reactionary politics or that he's often late to the mid-rise office building where you both work as janitors. It's not even that Jim occasionally forgets to swirl the toxic bleaching chemical in an alarming number of urinals, forcing Berthound, your imperious Albanian boss, to demand that you take up the slack.

No, the reason it's hard to work with Jim is because he's a grizzly bear. Nine and a half feet tall, and maybe 1,200 pounds, Jim towers over, well, everything. Mops, vacuum cleaners, the rotating marble-polisher you take turns sliding across the lobby's checker-board patterned floor—all are dwarfed in his massive paws.

Wrapped in his prickly pelt, Jim gripes and bitches his way through shift after endless shift, depleting the vending machine mercilessly and foraging loudly through the legal secretaries' desks for protein bars.

You can't say there haven't been some good times. Like when Jim got you and your girlfriend free tickets to see him ride a unicycle in the county fair. Or the currency of his information on where to get the freshest honey. But on the whole, Jim's been a challenging co-worker at best. Last spring's infamous basketball argument, for example, in which your support for Bill Russell over Hakeem Olajuwon as the best center to ever hit the hardwood, resulted in Jim rearing onto his hind legs and tossing a floor model photocopier across a conference room at your head, destroying several pieces of pricey designer office furniture in the bargain.

Tonight, however, when you arrive, having done your best to psych yourself up for another evening of cleaning toilets, wiping down desks and disposing of various accountant and lawyer trash, Jim is nowhere to be found. Not that Jim hasn't had troubles at work before. Last summer he was really down on himself for eating all the chocolate from the building's reception area instead of foraging for nuts and berries. And it's hard to count the number of times he's missed half a shift futilely hunting for spawning salmon in the small stream that bisects the office park.

It's Berthound who finally clues you in that Jim is hiding upstairs in the secret hallway leading to the freight elevator. Is it the hunters again, you wonder? Or is Jim expecting another visit from the animal rights people who want to sedate him and fly him by helicopter to a remote region of Minnesota where he will never again be able to watch his beloved Houston Rockets and instead be forced to listen to that nightmarish flattened O every time someone says the word "cola?"

But when you do eventually locate a shaking Jim cowering behind a dumpster, he tells you that due to substantial debts, it's actually Manny he's avoiding, his connection for the extra-strong methamphetamines he's been shooting since early November to avoid hibernation and its attendant weight gain, not to mention the squandering of his carefully-horded stash of sick, personal and vacation days.

COLOR SCHEME

THINK PINK!

Imagine a world in which everything is the glowing blush of a white man's balding, sunburned pate. From the roller skates to the window panes to the cassocks of the lonely, self-righteous priests. Each car, all the McMansions, the banks and the office parks, every single doggone miracle of nature that confronts you —every speck, every shard, insulation pink, Pink Panther pink, labial pink. Pink Cadillac pink.

You're trying. But you don't quite have it yet.

Really think pink!

The sky stretching out endlessly over the bent down head that sports your unhappy face is pink. The tempestuous ocean where you imagine your dreams will struggle briefly in the foam and chop before invariably sinking like stones is pink. The long curving roads—snaking through endless pink forests and pink fields and empty pink cities—all somehow leading to the same vast pink empire of nowhere are pink.

Everything but you. You are black. Black as a dark star. In America, this is what we call high school.

KAMPALA 2012

BLACK BOYS with skin the color of ebonite cradling automatic weapons that gleam like glass in the sun crowd the marketplace near the airport where the big jets still land. Their guns, it is said, carry bullets laved with the blood of radioactive animals poached out on the Kenyan border near one of the impact craters. Incanted over by the *sangoma*, these hollow points are rumored to bore through skin and bone, going straight for the heart of an enemy, devouring it and morphing instantaneously into harmless butterflies, yellow as margarine, light as air.

Dozens, perhaps hundreds, of these ghost insects haunt the warrens of wasteboard shacks south of the hospital, lighting on the grimy Panama hats of the white men and dappling the roofs of their Land Rovers calcium white with bug shit.

On nights of the full moon the lepidoptera swarm and luminesce under the mercury vapor lamps, singing the names of the dead. While the locals hide themselves within the moldering walls of their aluminum-roofed shacks—ears plugged with beeswax, lips offering sibilant prayers to ancestors long-vaporized—a man, never younger than seventy and always different, paces a slow circle at the widest crossroads for miles. He wears a necklace of blood orchids and shakes a rattle encasing the milk teeth of the eldest child from each family.

Although most suspect no real harm can come of hearing the butterflies trill the names of those who have passed, all are certain they would suffer irrevocably if the very old served no conspicuous and inarguable purpose. Wrinkled and forgetful as they are, these elders are their only link to the past, the only thing that keeps the boys in the marketplace from wanting to maintain an unbreakable hold on their shimmering guns long after they have grown into men.

JESUS IN 42

—for Leonard Cohen

JESUS CHRIST RIDES the Somerset Avenue streetcar into Windber, Pennsylvania, in the middle of the afternoon. It's early June, but a cool front stalled off the Great Lakes drives a stiff, ceaseless breeze keeping the temperature in the low 60s. This doesn't bother Jesus. In his grimy pit jacket, heavy denim pants and polystyrene kneepads, he is already prepared for a long night shoveling in the cold and damp underground.

What *is* driving the sweat on Jesus' upper lip, moistening his palms and making his heart dance a little faster than it ought, is that he is in real danger of being late for the afternoon shift at Mine 42. His crew boss is Mean Stiney Miller and Mean Stiney has told Jesus in no uncertain terms that if he's late again this month, it will mean a three-day suspension.

Jesus is in no position to afford three days without pay. His electric bill is overdue and both kids have "pay at time of service" doctor's appointments later this week. His wife is complaining she hasn't had her hair done in almost a month and it's starting to affect her tips at the Tipple Diner.

Jesus considers an appeal to his heavenly father to speed along the streetcar, slow time or give Stiney Miller's truck a flat tire on the winding dirt road from Elton.

Jesus is already flirting with unpopularity with the other miners on his crew. His long hair has been the subject of quite a few not entirely tasteful jokes concerning his sexuality and the soreness in his hands keeps him from being as adept with the pick as the other miners on his shift. Much to Jesus' embarrassment, he's been accused of "swinging the pick like a girl." And let's not even talk about the way the stitch in his side compromises his work with the coal shovel.

Snatching his lunch pail from the curved, plastic seat of the street car, Jesus breaks into a slow jog up the 18th Street hill, past Miner's Memorial Hospital. He's trying to hotfoot it past the showerhouse to his mantrip car at the mine's driftmouth before the screech of the shift whistle.

But when Christ arrives, sweat-stained and puffing, at the mine's entrance, the driftmouth is awash in activity. Miners are rushing toward the opening in the earth carrying coal shovels and blasting boxes. Freddie Pruchnic, the daylight crew boss, is calling for the fire boss and yelling for the tippleman to get the superintendent of the mine on the phone. Miners further back, near the fanhouse, are calling out to one another, asking what is happening. The voices of the men who have not seen the expression on Freddie's face are cautiously optimistic, hoping that whatever has taken place is bad enough that they will all be sent home with pay for the rest of the afternoon.

Jesus does not need to ask any of the frantic men what has occurred. He already knows that while cutting a coal pillar, Fat Tiny LaMonaca has misjudged the strength of the upper strata and has been buried in a cave-in two miles underground off the main shaft. Most of the ceiling of the giant underground room has collapsed and the way in is blocked by hundreds of tons of coal and dirty slate. Fat Tiny is just barely alive under the canopy of the coal cutting machine. His breath comes in gasps and his pulse is thready.

In minutes, the reinforced steel canopy of the coal cutter will crumble like newspaper under the weight of the seam and Fat Tiny's bones will be shattered into dust.

Short of a miracle, the fates of Fat Tiny and anyone in the chamber attempting a rescue are set in stone.

Stiney Miller bellows for his scrambling men to assemble themselves quick as shit on the seats of the yellow flatcar for the trip underground. Jesus stands frozen at the door of the powder shed. He does not want to take his place on the railcar. Jesus knows that depending on how fast Wally "The Wheelman" Stankevich can pilot the flatcar through the mine's slick, twisting track to the site of the collapse, there is a real chance they will arrive at the fork Fat Tiny was working as a second, more serious phase of the cave-in occurs and the mine's roof gives the whole way back to the main shaft.

"Hey, Christ," Mean Stiney shouts to Jesus. "Shake a leg."

Sorely conflicted, Jesus watches dozens of miners swarm to the growing line of mantrip cars, their rescue packs large and heavy across their backs, their expressions grim and jaws set. Jesus knows any action but rushing to his seat on the railcar, rescue pack slung over his shoulder and short shovel in hand, will mark him forever a coward and a traitor to his fellow miners. His ostracism will be instant, irremediable and complete. Even his children will have no hope of escaping social sanction bordering on banishment in its severity.

One booted foot in the powder shed and the other on the cracked concrete slab leading back to the railyard, Jesus mumbles a fervent prayer into the filthy sleeve of his pit jacket.

"Please take," he whispers, "this cup from me."

Nervously, Jesus waits as the long, empty seconds tick by. But of course there is no answer—no one there even to answer.

Jesus shrugs.

With a quick step back into the powder shed, Jesus retrieves a ten-weight tempered steel pry bar from behind the outbuilding's plank door. Threading the snarl of anxious, quick-moving men, Jesus slips through the railyard and two-at-a-times the greasy, coal-slick steps to the top of the control platform for the mine's power feeds.

Poised in front of the electric panels apportioning power to the mine's tipple belts and flatcars, Jesus feels any possible future in the town fade slowly and vanish. Joylessly resigned to acting out his singular destiny, Jesus slams the pry bar into the cover of the distribution box controlling the power feeds for flatcars entering the mine.

By the third strike the sheet metal cover hangs limply from the box and its electronic guts are spread through the railyard like leaves after an autumn blow. Not a single soul will be flatcar-ring into Mine 42 now, not for hours, not until the assembly has been rebuilt by a mine electrician brought in from Wheeling.

Slackjawed, miners stare at Christ as he, prybar lowered to his side, walks slowly out from behind the bank of switch boxes and down the corrugated stairs from the operations deck.

Their throats awash in curses, the men from Jesus' crew—men he has known his whole life—drop their rescue packs and raise their shovels. Howling, these grim-faced men rush at him from across the railyard, calling for vengeance, calling for blood.

ICE WATER, HERE ON EARTH

—for Yaseen Nabeel

ON FRIDAYS, the Muslim women wept. Lavish tears in the swirling shapes of black abayas, these plunging arabesques of sadness and want fell to the dry earth and saturated the empty clay streets of Damascus.

On Saturdays, the Jewish women took their turn, expelling their doubt and regret in aqueous beads one after the next, puddling the ancient avenues from St. Paul's to Saladin's Tomb.

On Sundays, the Christian women's terrific hopelessness and sense that all had gone irremediably wrong welled up and expended itself in gigantic cruciform tears filling the plazas and coating the travertine patios, till some of the devout began to question whether it would, in fact, be fire next time.

But Monday mornings the streets of Damascus were solemn and quiet and all that could be heard was the soft slicing of the atheists' ice skate blades as they zipped across the vast rink of chilled sadness that had formed overnight—that and of course their whistling, sibilant and tuneful, as if every empty block through which they axeled and lutzed were a graveyard.

A USER'S GUIDE TO BRINGING MY EX-GIRLFRIEND SHELLEY TO ORGASM

1. Get a job. Preferably not one at the lumber mill or with the fire department in a small town in rural Oregon where you'll learn from men who haven't been laid in years to refer to the great majority of women as broads or twats even when they're standing around listening to you say this. Of course, any form of employment, no matter how marginal or temporary, is more effective than simply sitting at home on your ass watching reruns of Bass Master Challenge on cable and slugging down Evan Williams with a lemonade back.

2. Stop mentioning "maybe trying out a threesome" with her friend Becky who works down at Charlene's House of Hair on Commerce Street. This is especially important if Becky has just come back from her spring vacation in one of those Florida towns called Beach Something and she's got a deep tan and can't stop telling everyone about her new piercing "down there."

3. Insistence on listening to a cassette copy of your cousin's cover band work its way through side one of *Steve Miller's Greatest Hits* while the two of you get busy isn't going to do you any favors.

4. Remember to call her "Shelley" *every* time you're doing it, no matter how desperately you might be pretending she's really Heather Locklear or the new checkout girl at Family Dollar with the boob job. (Note: a slipup here can really cost you, not only in the moment, but in opportunities to try again for at least a month —cause no matter how big your junk is, it ain't reaching nothing from the living room couch, *essè*.)

5. Keep the nightstand drawer stocked with extra heavy duty batteries. And when she reaches for them, don't mention how they were pocketed from Family Dollar while the new girl, "y'know, the one with the boob job," was flirting with you, because why pay when you don't have to, especially with money being so tight and all—and oh, yeah, she should probably know that the grocery money you didn't blow at the dog track got traded to a high school kid named Snake for an eighth of purple hair hydroponic and no, there isn't a whole lot left.

6. When, as a last resort, she quotes you one of those "women's books" that encourage honest communication between couples, it's guaranteed your surly remarking, "What the hell's taking so long? My last girlfriend could have had three by now!" *will* get your broke ass tossed out of her singlewide and into the chilly Oregon night with zest and suddenness, especially after your initial attempt at forthright communication involved the observation that her recent weight gain could probably be shed more easily if she stopped choking down a pint of Häagen-Dazs Almond Hazelnut Swirl in front of the Hallmark channel every night and maybe joined the fitness center across from the fire hall and of course she shouldn't feel self-conscious—a lot of bigger girls have started going there now that the broad who used to run the place quit and moved her uppity twat back to goddamned Portland where she belongs.

LIFE LESSON

IT'S 1972 and the war, unpopular now even in the suburbs, sputters on. My father, not a Buddhist monk, nonetheless flirts with self-immolation. Slumped on our blacktop drive next to the Roadmaster, he's poured a quart of Fleischmann's gin down the front of his chest. His left hand toys with the wheel of a Zippo. "Alice," he shouts to my mother. "Alice, get out here." When my mom, beehive blond and rayon-ed, comes rustling through the screen door, he smears some of the gin into his hair, a splash across his whiskery face. "Have this baby," he tells her, "I swear I'll go up like Dresden." Even as my mother sprays him down with the garden hose, calls for my uncle in the house across the street, my father is laughing. "I can do this any time, Alice," he says.

THE GIRL WITH THE MOST CAKE

AFTER THE DEATH of her father at a hospital that was not Cedars-Sinai, the compact blond girl with tits like cantaloupes decamped Reseda for a low-slung, anonymous apartment in Studio City shared with a man who described his occupation as sound engineer. The man never seemed to engineer any sounds, except yelling at the neighbors for the way they parked their expensive German motorcycle too close to his car, but he liked to have an underage girl or two around when he went to meetings at Capitol Records or to clubs like the Viper Room on Sunset Boulevard. Mostly though, they would slump on the sofa in front of his flat screen TV and eat takeout Hawaiian pizza from the California Pizza Kitchen and watch old music videos. The girl liked the pizza, which somehow seemed tastier in the Studio City apartment, but after a few weeks of the man's snarky comments about "kids today" she could feel resentment budding in her chest. The girl tried to ignore the twinge and listen to his vast store of knowledge about key changes, vocal compression and Phil Spector's wall of sound. Sometimes she would accompany the sound engineer on meet and greets where she would smile and nod and try to pick up a few things.

When she met the music producer who drove the bone

white Range Rover at the coffee bar on Vermont Avenue in Los Feliz, she was pretty sure he was one of the things she wanted to pick up. After a quick conversation in which dazzling teeth were flashed and adoration displayed, the girl returned to the anonymous apartment in Studio City. She collected her things, called for a taxi.

In the music producer's house she had her own bedroom. She had a window that looked down into Nichols Canyon and a small refrigerator that held more pomegranate juice than she could ever imagine drinking. She spent her late-starting days in the music producer's small office on Little Santa Monica Boulevard breaking appointments and telling low-level recording executives that the music producer was not shooting whiskey, was not snorting cocaine, that things were under control. Nights, the two of them would sit Indian style on a capacious microfiber sofa from the Armani Home Store on Melrose and the music producer would take white pills and lie to dozens of people on the phone one after the other. Later, he would feed her Thai food from cardboard cartons and complain that young people always want the reward before the work.

"Nothing personal," he would tell her.

The girl would nod and dump more pad Thai onto the brightly-colored Emile Henry plates the man would eventually ask her to fetch from the kitchen. She enjoyed the savory tang of pad Thai, but his self-indulgence rankled and she figured she'd best keep her eyes open.

By the time she married, the compact blond girl had fretted in a cottage in the Bird Streets above Sunset Plaza with an aging casting director, shared a gaudy neo- Georgian that bulged the edges of a quarter acre Rodeo lot with an unscrupulous talent agent and listened to the surf until she thought she would scream with a famously obsessive cinematographer in a post and beam north of Malibu.

After the ceremony, she finally trucked the contents of her rented Beachwood Canyon bungalow to a glass fortress on

Zoroaster Drive so far above LA there wasn't even pollution. Here, she would continue her work as the head of a production company for her new husband, an A-list action film director who slept on an oversized circular bed in a room down the hall.

Mere days after the decorator positioned her slatted Nelson benches at an obtuse angle that forced guests to observe the house's full-on canyon views, the compact blond girl overheard the director plotting to hire someone else to head up the production company, a much younger girl with tits the size of honeydews and eyes like shiny almonds, whom some lowlife at the Polo Lounge had recommended as a giver of especially tantalizing blow jobs. The compact blond girl spent several hours pacing the narrow, cantilevered deck off her bedroom looking out at Santa Catalina. Wringing her hands and thinking back on all she'd experienced since leaving the smog and acid washed jeans of Reseda, she had a realization. Here is what she realized: The size of the cake only matters when it's your cake.

That night she slipped into the voluminous marble master bath and reloaded each of her husband's blood pressure capsules with a double dose of Viagra. Over a breakfast of pomegranate juice and egg whites, she warned each of the female assistants in turn about an upcoming round of brutal budget cuts, sternly informing them that fucking her husband in some lame attempt to keep their jobs would never, never work.

Now months later, having managed the small, tasteful funeral, the reading of the will, the public service at Forest Lawn and a suitable period of mourning, the blond girl winds a graphite Aston Martin down the narrow canyon streets to take meetings at the Ivy on Robertson. She tells them to do this and she tells them to do that—and she eats dessert happily, happily ever after.

TEN FACTS ABOUT FIRE

1. Fire is often used as a metaphor—generally suggesting creativity, passion and occasionally, insanity.

2. Fire consumes irrevocably what it burns.

3. The implications of Fact Two should always be kept in mind whenever one states, regarding feelings for a new lover, words to the effect of, "I'm burning for you." This is particularly true when addressing a woman one will later think of as "my ex-wife" and later yet, "my first wife."

4. Fire is self-replicating.

5. A long-winded interrogation of the ramifications of Fact One in a doctoral dissertation on Nabokov will *not* be regarded as a coup—and may play a substantial part in one's ending up teaching a 5/5 load of composition courses at a junior college in an especially unglamorous city in the middle west.

6. Fire is almost without fail accompanied by smoke.

7. If the smoke happens to be the result of burning marijuana that your teenage son has rolled into Zig-Zag cigarette papers and set ablaze and the state police are the ones doing the smelling following a traffic stop, they will not care that Fact Six is a clever qualification of a well-recognized proverb coined by said teenage son the night before the SAT to defuse household tension after the smoke detector has once again functioned as the family dinner bell.

8. "Fire!" was the main catchphrase employed by a character named Beavis on animator Mike Judge's popular, satirical, early-to-mid-nineties cartoon "Beavis and Butthead."

9. When your eldest daughter's shouting of this moldering catch-phrase during an experiment in a high school chemistry class results in a classmate's broken arm as the students flee the smoke-filled lab and Laura's subsequent suspension adds, slightly but critically, to the household's already untenable amount of tension, you may noticeably hesitate—just a crucial once—when continually asked by said daughter, "Is it my fault you're fighting?"

10. When it is your house going up in a wall of blistering orange flame and you can do nothing but stand outside after the divorce in the swirling red glow of the light from the trucks and smell the smoke coming off your bathrobe and give thanks your dog is still alive and your kids weren't home, Facts Four and Two gain nearly unimaginable weight and currency, while Fact One becomes almost instantly less relevant than a distant star gone dark right around the time dinosaurs, unchallenged, ruled the earth.

THIS IS NOT A STORY ABOUT LAST CHANCES

I REMEMBER the night you brought home the dog. It was three a.m. and I had to get up for breakfast with my boss to discuss the quarter's paltry sales numbers. Because the garage door opener was on the fritz and you felt strongly that you had to get the dog into the basement (couldn't leave it in the convertible, it might jump out) you had to sequester our shepherd in the bedroom. I woke the first time when you opened the door and shoved Bart inside—whining and nails scraping on the hardwood—so you could coax the stray through the house.

I often wonder about the meaning of your rescuing the dog that night. Did waking me like that signify you already regarded our marriage as effectively over? Was it important that you were on your way home from the night shift at the restaurant and not some bar? Was, perhaps, the dog a talisman for you? Were you trying to save yourself by saving the dog? Trying to save us by jumping out of the car to rescue the dog from the middle of a busy freeway south of Echo Park?

After the dog bit you on the back porch and ran off yapping into the woods and I had to get up to drive you to the emergency room before dawn, maybe I could have opened my heart and fallen back in love as you slumped in the passenger seat, eyes drooping and a dishtowel wrapped around your bloody hand, but all I could see—and you pushed me to wear these blinders, I swear—was another acrobatic morning and splashes of red fixing to the car seat.

SHOOTING ELVIS

WHEN I LIVED on the Lower East Side in the late-seventies, my downstairs neighbor, Regina, used to play Elvis Presley records every time she shot up heroin. Love Me Tender, Don't Be Cruel, (You Ain't Nothin' But a) Hound Dog. I could hear these shitty, scratched-to-hell Elvis 45s blaring up through the floor every weekend. Sometimes I'd go down to complain. Sometimes I'd say, "Goddamn, Reg. Quit playing them fucking Elvis records." But she'd just stare up at me with this glassy, far away, fucked-up look in her eyes, tapping a blackened tablespoon against the arm of her ratty cotton couch.

After a while, all I ever heard was Elvis, all the time. Day and night. Night and day. Well, I knew what that meant. Then it stopped. The next time I saw Regina, I told her I figured it was good that she quit shootin' heroin. I told her that fuckin' Elvis croon at all hours was starting to drive me batshit. She looked up at me with a dazed expression. Said she'd pawned the record player for ten bucks. Asked me if I knew anyone who'd be interested in buying some Elvis records, cheap.

SHOWING WALTER'S HOUSE

LOOKIE-LOO'S or ready-to-buy's with checkbook in hand, the first thing any of them want to see—if they're in possession of all the facts—is never the fenced-in yard or the new Sub-Zero appliances in the freshly tiled kitchen or even the small stainless steel accented deck with a view of the harbor that juts out from the master suite. Would-be buyers don't care about the wide plank flooring or the state-of-the-art security system. They could be watching paint dry when I point to where the nonstructural wall used to be and how the house is one of the city's prime examples of Federalist architecture adapted for modern living.

Without exception, potential purchasers head straight for the bathroom. They let their noses fill with the scents of Pine-Sol and bleach and tentatively—always tentatively—run their hands along the tile walls. Their eyes linger on the chromed water pipe running across the ceiling to the shower.

Invariably, their gazes fix on the slight crook near the center, where, I understand, the extension cord was tied. Then they unfailingly tell me, "Thanks, but no. I don't think I could live in a place where something like this happened."

AB INITIO!

—with thanks to Hannah Bottomy

HURRICANE of Sikorsky blades splashes sand across the tarmac centered dark in the desert like a poison oasis and Pfc Shemansky humps his M60 into the dazzle, coughs up phlegm, curses his first sergeant, the hadjis and life in general before striking out on a quick recon run six clicks south of Ramadi.

BEFORE THAT greasy Terrazzo floor. Kandinsky of bright blood. Big, square-shouldered kid hauling ass up 16th Street in the late autumn drizzle, knuckles abraded to bleeding, scarlet-stained letterman jacket, a plea of "guilty with an explanation," and conception of himself as someone forever impulsive and doomed setting in his mind like quick-dry cement.

BEFORE THAT urged on by a Greek chorus of Stomp That Wetback!, a lithe, mocha body is flung across the counter, yanked off the floor and a frightened, high cheek-boned face gets punched twice by a weight-trained football player's clenched fist before a jet shock of hair is grabbed and a face is shoved forward, smacked hard enough to crunch bone against the rounded Formica corner of a four top piled high with McFlurrys and Big Macs.

BEFORE THAT an overworked, brown-skinned coun-
terman mistakes Odie Shemansky (blond, blue-eyed quarterback) for Eddie Stankevich (blond, blue-eyed cornerback) and
instead of presenting him his customary double cheeseburger
with extra pickles, no onions, no ketchup and just a little
mustard, exchanges his $3.45 for a large coke and a sundae with
extra peanuts, to which Odie is deathly allergic. Words pass. The
sundae is bank shot into the deep fryer. Odie the Quarterback is
called a "cocksucker."

BEFORE THAT Odie fails geometry, social studies and
earth science, exposing him to a fusillade of caustic remarks
about his ever-diminishing chances of "amounting to shit" from
his alcoholic father that ravage his limited self-worth, already
near gutted last week by the record four interceptions thrown in
the season's final game against tiny, single A Portage, the
crowning ignominy of Windber High's first winless season since
1970—all of which only served to further compound the hopelessness and self-doubt magnified by Odie's recent discovery that
his last girlfriend, Alyssa Moskowitz, has not only given head to
the point guard of the basketball team in the back seat of a
Dodge Charger while drunk at the Scalp Fire Hall's Fall Carni-
val, but laughingly told everyone who'd listen that she only did it
because she wanted to have at least one experience before she
turned 18 with a guy who didn't have a "pencil pecker."

BEFORE THAT the oldest son of the first Mexican family
to move to Windber, Pennsylvania, scrawls his Enrico Martinez
in loopy, girl-like cursive onto the signature line of the applica-
tion for employment of the 16th Street McDonald's, aiming to
help the family pay the race-inflated rent on their Scalp Level
duplex after his father, Carlito, is laid off from his job as a diesel
mechanic at the Chevy dealership on Marhefka Boulevard,
when business takes a nosedive due to gas prices.

BEFORE THAT Stanley Shemansky, functioning alcoholic,
is laid off from United States Steel's Twelve Inch Mill for
twenty-four out of the last thirty months of his son Odie's dwin-

dling adolescence, and fed up with having no health insurance and feeding his kids Ramen Noodles most nights, punctuates his boys' weekly beatings with the admonition that they better wise up, get some kind of damn education, because between the wetbacks sneaking under the fence from Mexico and the dirty Japs and Chinks undercutting every single thing we used to make here, unless the boys can scare up a goddamn PhD, they might just as well toss their dumb asses off the rusting Babcock Trestle or run out and join the stinking army.

OBLIATION

PENNY MASTURBATED. Standing in the shower with her legs akimbo and her eyes locked on the intersection of four particularly clean squares of cornflower blue ceramic tile, she touched herself. She felt the water crash into her shoulders, her breasts, the taut, pasty skin stretched across her belly. The steam billowed up around her and evanesced in slow waves where it met the bathroom's shabby drop ceiling.

She had been teasing for a long while and knew only a few minutes of hot water were left before a mountain stream of cold punctured her reverie like a roadside bomb. Summoning, she slid her finger across her clit, closed her eyes.

As always, she imagined Odie in the desert, his bright almond eyes and square-jawed face sweaty and windburned beneath a patina of dirt and sand. He has stopped the insurgents' four-wheel drive on the narrow dirt road on the sandy outskirts of Ramadi. Again, they fail to present him with the appropriate papers. In his clear, loud, quarterback's voice, he orders them both out of the vehicle. The one in the passenger's seat—a grubby little fart of a man, turbaned and greasy, with a nasty curl to his dark mouth—furtively reaches behind the narrow bucket seat, raises an oil black .45 caliber pistol. He fires pointblank at

Odie and while the gunshot is tremendous, plangent across the expanse of desert, the round whizzes past Odie's full, smooth lips, leaving him unscathed, but justified in his erupting fury. Odie slaps the composite plastic butt of his M-16 into the man's largish nose, unleashing a fierce burst of blood. The gun butt's second strike snaps the man's cheekbones like the skeleton of a bird caught in an industrial fan. His thick, ropey muscles straining beneath his BDUs, Odie beats this man, then the other, until their faces give like mush. By the time she imagines Odie radioing the first sergeant staffing the checkpoint at the city center, Penny has come so hard, her legs have given way and she's cross-legged on the polyvinyl floor and cold water roars out of the showerhead soaking her like January rain.

Toweling her narrow back in front of the space heater, Penny is both horrified and secretly proud of the harshness and dark violence of this fantasy—but she's not worried. As long as she imagines every detail exactly the same, this magic can't fail.

Her beautiful Odie, he'll stay safe.

FABLE OF THE DECONSTRUCTION #23: TEXT, CONTEXT AND SUBTEXT WALK INTO A BAR

A BAR?

♠ "Hold up, motherfucker!" scowls Text. "A bar? How can anyone walk *into* a bar? A bar clearly suggests a barrier to entry, something through which one cannot pass. To 'bar' the way is obviously to block it. We are *not* walking into a bar. End of story! You couldn't *give* away the rights to this narratological mess."

♣ "Barrier to entry? That's all you got for us, Text?" says Subtext. "Man, you've turned punk since Derrida! What about a bar of music? Prison bars? Passing the bar? The Iso bars of pressure that daily wilt and wreck my precious calm? Not to mention the low lit barracoon we've just entered where gallons of beautiful liquor reflect dimly in an aging silver mirror, this subterranean lair where I plan to get so deep in my cups, I'll need a life jacket. Who let the dogs out? Subtext let the dogs out! Bourbon and water till I'm boiled as an owl!"

♦ "I don't hear color bar!" enjoins Context. "Don't *let* me think you two are not considering the ramifications of the color bar. Had the color bar not been enforced below the Mason-Dixon line until the freedom rides, street protests and the 'about damn time' court decisions of the civil rights era, our parents could have enjoyed this fine drinking establishment, absenting themselves from our tedious adolescence in a blur of loose knit, tipsy narrative and leather banquette debauchery reminiscent of Fitzgerald."

♦ ♣ ♠ "Color bar. Right, baby," all promptly accede. They swill mightily, still congenitally contentious, but satiate in the lubricated, easy now.

Stay tuned for:
Fable of the Deconstruction #43:
Born Under a Bad Signifier: Jim from Critical Theory 2012

BOB IN THE CROSSHAIRS

Cheryl

Our first date was a humid Friday night in late spring and Bob took me to see his uncle's band play at the Polish Falcon's Nest. The weather was warm for that time of year and we sweat through our clothes moving around the high-ceilinged room to songs like the "Beer Barrel Polka" and "That'll Be the Day." I liked how his muscles bulged his tight collar and tapered sleeves, the way his big hands held me through the damp, clinging cotton of my blouse as we spun on the sawdusted wooden floor. During the slow numbers, I let him pull me in close. I stared up into his coffee-colored eyes, watched the curve of his thick lips. I adored the way his pomade-darkened hair stayed shellacked in place, except for an inky squiggle that dangled over his forehead like it was taking a dare.

Outside, I noticed the welding scars on his wrists and forearms when he leaned in to kiss me. His chest felt solid against my splayed palm, reassuring, but his tongue was too big for my mouth and I could smell the sweat souring on his shirt in the night air. I told him my dad needed me home before eleven and started for the passenger door of his Dodge, leaving him standing with his thick arm on the brick wall of the Falcon's, cigarette burning away to nothing.

Lois

I could tell right away he didn't belong in Principles of Modern Accounting any more than a golden retriever belongs in command of missile defense for the European Theatre—but there he sat, hunched in the second row, coveralls stained black, cigarette behind his ear, gnawed pencil between his fingers week after week, look of confusion on his face so intent we all assumed his first language was something quite unrelated to English, at least until the soggy afternoon around midterms when he cocked his hip and asked me for a light.

He told me he owned a garage out on the highway and had taken the class to get up to speed on the billing since his wife left him high and dry the year before. The first night he drove me out there, he put the moves on me right away, throwing his arm around my shoulder as we drove, his hand brushing the swell of my breast.

We only ever slept together in his garage nights after class when my sister thought I was mastering the intricacies of monetary unit assumption with the ladies' study group. Each time we did it, he bent me over the quarter panel of a car in for repairs, a Pontiac or a Chevy. He'd call me a "dirty bitch" and worse the whole time we were screwing. It excited me that he actually seemed very angry when we did it, like I was a stand-in for everything that was wrong with the world. It was flattering to be focused on so intently. It kept me coming back for a while. After the semester break, when we didn't see each other for a few weeks, I thought I might need some kind of therapy and when I saw his number on the caller ID, I let the phone ring and ring.

Jo

No matter what you've heard, nothing much happened between us. Not, at least, until the middle of his divorce proceedings. Even then it wasn't much. Twice. Maybe, three times. He'd toy with the hem of my skirt as I sat on the edge of my desk while we went over the testimony he'd give the judge. He'd grouse about how unhappy he'd been with his wife, talk up his experiences with other women. He'd compliment the smell of my dark hair, the cut of my dresses, the curve of my ass. Some nights he'd rest his hand on my knee. One night when I was pissed at Karl for not paying me enough attention, I let it stay there.

I'm well aware, however, small towns never offer generous allowances of discretion for outsiders. It isn't a long journey—maybe only from the corner bar to the coffee shop—before lawyers, especially married ones, who don't have their own trove of secrets to raise as a bulwark against rumor, become the butt of sexual appetite jokes, at least for the few trying months that precede the rigors of a disbarment hearing.

Martha

Thursdays were my nights. I'd press the buzzer for his apartment over the Tipple Tavern and he'd let me in. We'd sit on the bed and swig Budweiser from cold brown bottles, watch television till Leno, then screw standing up. The first time I found panties two sizes too small bunched under the bed, I told him I wouldn't be back. The second time, I learned I might be the kind of woman who puts up with that sort of thing and he was the sort of man who would let me.

Caroline

My father's kidney problems aren't the root of his meanness, but I'm hoping they become the root of my forgiveness. The winding, meditative drive to Dave's Dialysis grants us the dubious blessing of proximity. His rheumy eyes twitch in their dark sockets taking in the coal country landscape like a punishment.

In the waiting room, I read *Family Circle* or *Redbook*, think about what to make for dinner, imagine my mother in her patterned apron and bouffant pulling a tray of steaming *haluski* from the oven as we wait at the Formica table in the kitchen of our frame house on Sixth Street, sour look on her broad face suggesting tolerance pushed hours too far into the night and faltering. I picture my father reclined on the chilly table inside, shriveled body badged with the titanium intake valve that saves his life every week. I try to decide if my mother were still alive, would she be grateful?

Sometimes on the way back to my father's ranch house off the highway we'll stop at the Valley Dairy on Dark Shade Drive. He'll order an egg white omelet with turkey bacon, slash his eyes sideways and joke with the waitress about the weather, the football team. On these mornings when he's full of clean blood, I'll want to ask him about the women that took him away from us, ask him if they were worth breaking our hearts, but instead I sit quietly in the booth, watch him chew his eggs like they're beefsteak.

POSSESSIONS

IN THE DREAM, it's Marley's last concert. September 1980. The crush and swirl of Pittsburgh's Stanley Theatre—the mill-workers, the waitresses, the stockboys, the slick- haired lawyers—all on their feet and swinging pale hands through the air, beckoning for the encore, their cheers cajoling the great, ailing man back onto the wide plank stage. Forty, maybe fifty rows back, the people who surround you are unfamiliar. You bob and weave like a boxer ducking trouble trying to keep your gaze fixed on Marley's penduluming dreads as he moves between stacks of speakers, musicians whose names you don't know.

When the gears catch, Marley is seated. His guitar balanced across his thinning legs, he is already at the song's piercing chorus. Rhythmic and voluble, the music is sweetness itself, notes rising through the vast room like a benediction. His eyes deep set and tired, almost pleading, Marley is asking the crowd if they will help him to sing. The people surrounding you hold small butane flames at shoulder level like tiny campfires quavering toward unity. Not entirely on key, they warble and drone back to Marley that, just like him, *Redemption Songs are all they ever have*. It is a moment of pure connection. Oneness. So perfect and so near you can almost feel the warm hand of god reaching down from fresh heaven and cupping your heart in its glowing, numinous palm.

But you are not singing. Not swaying. You have no butane lighter to hold. While your heart acknowledges the implacable pull of the moment, you feel only its transience and cliché. Your inability to connect here is profound, inviolable. There is nothing you will take home but a headshaking puzzlement at the hokiness and showbiz of the whole affair. This is it, you remember. This is the dream in which you are alone.

$4,500

"NOPE," said the foreman. "Won't be the jury gets hung, that's all you can lay hands on."

BRUCE REDMAN SAYS "NO, BUT MAYBE"

WHILE AS A RULE more than ready to cash in on developing the antics for *Survivor: Next Generation, The Bronx*—the spectacular, if unused, "Bumfight Immunity Challenge" in particular —and being in a bit of a pickle (well, really more of a Mexican prison) myself right now—I still must decline your production company's offer to function as show runner for next season.

I don't dispute that *Survivor: Armageddon* represents a potential high-octane ratings smash. The sun-seared, post-apocalyptic hellscape you propose as setting should continue to reinvigorate and extend the *Survivor* brand. But I find it unconscionable to profit from exploding a five-kiloton nuclear device eight miles inside the low population density Central Asian republic the network's marketing team has so trenchantly accorded the sobriquet, Trashcanistan. Or, should I say, I find it unconscionable to profit to such a *limited degree*.

Now, should your proffered, niggardly compensation—likely deemed generous by the gaggle of shit-for-brains entertainment lawyers responsible for concocting your turd of a deal memo—be suitably, i.e., *substantially*, increased, then you may Count! Me! In!

As I suspect your will to maintain a position of ersatz penury will wilt like a post-coital prick, I've taken the liberty to limn a few ideas I believe vital to next season's ratings catching, uh, fire.

First and foremost, a mushroom cloud credit sequence is imperative. Only by starting things off with a bang (well, actually more of a 400 hexadecible all-consuming roar able to drown out a car crash or domestic dispute forty kilometers away on the pocked boulevards of Bishkek) can we really guarantee our audience that we've raised *Survivor*'s stakes in a manner that truly commands attention on a global scale. Next, I see fighter jets—F-19s, MiGs, Raptors, whatever we can get—a whole flock of them performing an aerial Busby Berkeley number as the blast's initial shock wave vaporizes huts, cattle, villagers, insects, bicycles, toothpaste, Holy Qu'rans, MP-3 players, dandruff, everything more or less within approximately two miles.

Of course, the most intriguing aspect of your proposal is not so much the exponential increase in the number of contestants, but the involuntary nature of their participation. Detonating the nuclear device above the dun-colored outskirts of the tiny, arid village of Pokortova at dawn without warning ought to net us at minimum no fewer than 300 *actual* survivors—providing at least six separate narrative strands to follow throughout the season. My only suggestion here is that we do our best to time the explosion for 8:59 pm Eastern Time on the first Thursday during the November sweeps.

Furthermore, the season's arc must take into account that no more than fifty percent of those who live through the blast's initial effects can reasonably be expected to "survive" beyond a 15 to 25 day window. While radiation poisoning certainly represents the most serious threat to the affected populace, a lack of potable water and comestibles should not be discounted when attempting to establish a baseline mortality rate. We should see some amazing tear-jerker moments here: suppurating villagers consoling each other as they perish due to a heartbreaking lack of proper medical care. That being said, those participants exposed to more than forty-five grays of radiation will be voted off this plane of existence in the very first episode.

Additionally, the "radiation sickness challenge" you propose as the meat and potatoes of the inaugural episode should, I suspect, be pushed to somewhat later in the season. Instead, an early episode could hinge on the finding of an immunity idol in the form of a radiation suit or medical treatment for the beta radiation burns sure to be lacerating the lungs of the poor suckers nearest the epicenter of the blast.

Moreover, while we don't want to miss the nausea and vomiting that accompanies radiation sickness, I'd suggest taping episodes three and four during the 48-hour radiation sickness latency period—thus allowing the home audience to build sympathy for the contestants prior to their becoming puking, shitting messes.

Your suggestion to employ Henry Kissinger as the first "Celebrity Host" does demonstrate a certain moxie, but may be problematic, as I suspect few viewers under the age of 55 will be able to recognize the former Secretary of State. Instead, I propose we reach out to North Korean dictator Kim Jong-un. Clearly a win-win, this represents needed time on the world stage for the diminutive autocrat and could provide us with inimical color commentary on inflicting mass suffering from someone to whom it's really no stranger.

Finally, whether or not I choose to come on board for *Survivor: Armageddon*, I must voice a most strenuous objection to the alternate concept floated in last Tuesday's development Skype session. As I expect little to no meaningful progress will be made to contain the Ebola virus before pilot season, *Survivor Outbreak* is the kind of project in which I can only see myself participating if my compensation package were to include not only an organized jailbreak (it worked for El Chapo!) but also the entire island of Santa Catalina and a phalanx of heavily armed troops in biohazard suits. Of course this would likely put you well over budget—particularly as the catastrophic population loss in nearly all key demographics would ratfuck any and all chances whatever of achieving our real, mutual goal here: syndication.

STRIPPER

HER MOUTH IS like a Fifties song—one of those clattering salvos from when rock and roll was black leather and boots and only half a step removed from the reformatory— angry and caught up in being demonstrative about it. Tight as a bass line trails a backbeat, her sneer eases only to talk sex in a sly, aggressive way, hint of a drawl lingering like the smoke in a basement room filled with angry, tattooed boys whose breath—all whiskey and Lucky Strike straights—advertises their fever pitch self-destructive proclivities, but that's just fine with the girl with the rockabilly mouth because nobody in this dark room tensing muscles or talking about jail is half as impelled toward self-obliteration. No one else's pockets bulge with needle bleach or retrovirals and nobody sports track marks between their toes or under a long-sleeved shirt that's about to get flung over a lamp when the lights dim and the booty-shake comes up and then flush with hatred for her own pale body, the defiant rail thin girl gives each nipple a hard twist and spins up from the wasteland of a couch launching into the same careening striptease that's been paying her rent since decamping art school last year. Moving as if she hears secret music, silky smooth and junkyard mean, the girl grinds her skinny ass till she feels blessed in a complex, brutal way, finally letting her mouth slacken into a dazed smile—just like Toulouse-Lautrec, she thinks, stumbling the uneven streets of Paris, paint on his hands, veins luminous with inspiration and syphilis.

SHOPPING

HER THROAT LOOSE-SKINNED AND PALE, rounded by a necklace of living snakes—diamondbacks, the patinas of their hourglasses fluorescing under the humming lights, and vipers, mouths agog, venom dripping—the widow rushes into Galeries Lafayette.

Her quick eyes futilely search one glass case after another, scanning wildly until she corrals a copper-skinned salesgirl near the perfume counter.

"I am here to purchase grace," the widow announces.

The tawny salesgirl, reveling in the rare opportunity of having the upper hand, says haughtily, "You cannot buy grace here. You are rich and have led a life overfull of privilege. There is no grace I can sell you."

"What do you know about it?" the widow replies. "It's true, I was rich. But my husband beat me and my children were full of spite."

"That is no concern of mine. Did you have no choice but to stay? Did your husband's beatings make you give more money to the poor? Did his rain of open-handed blows across your white face open your heart to the lonely? Did your children's bile push you to live with an eye to service? No, I can no more sell you grace than I could sell you my youth or you sell me your ruined, white skin."

Bending at the waist, the widow leans over the glass counter arrayed with vials and tubes. She scowls, and as her unblinking eyes dart from one container to the next, one of the snakes strikes the salesgirl on the tip of her slightly-wide nose. She falls dead behind a pyramid-shaped display of sapphire blue bottles.

Unruffled, the widow steps over the salesgirl's brown, cooling body. She rummages through the bottles, flinging one after another over her shoulder, infuriating the department store's well-heeled clientele.

"I had no choice. I had no choice," the widow shouts minutes later, her arms fixed behind her back as the uniformed security guards march her out into the street, careful to avoid the serpents' marauding fangs, still seeking, still dripping.

THREE REAL FAST

Salesman's Last Pitch

Cadillac Bob's nitroglycerin tablets rest useless as truth in the shiny jacket crumpled in the back seat of a late model Camaro. Until they don't, his customers assume his contortions a gimmick.

Picayune Matchmaker Classified

Topped by new composition roofs, the Marigny shotguns cried out for tenants. Hungry and busted, months after the water, hours away, we wept for houses.

LA Fitness, Bridgeville, Pa.

After the shooting started, I was thankful at every pop. Not me. Not me. Not me. Then, finally, thank Christ, him

.

THE WORST THING THAT CAN HAPPEN IS WHAT'S HAPPENING RIGHT NOW

IT'S Saturday afternoon and for reasons in no real way germane to what's about to unfold, I am sitting in the crowded second floor dining room of a McDonald's in Bay Ridge, Brooklyn—the Deep South of Brooklyn. Across the room, a man my age—mid-thirties—trim and muscular, cocks his hip to one side and clenches his jaw.

He looms, quietly seething above a woman in a rumpled, powder blue jogging suit whose dull hair and lumpy body evidence too many meals like this one. The woman is trying to coerce a screaming, strollered child into holding on to a small stuffed penguin. The penguin is missing a foot, and the child, a girl, maybe three, keeps flinging the tattered animal down onto the grimy terrazzo floor.

The quietly seething man wears newish, expensive sneakers, but his hair needs cutting and his pants are baggy, bargain basement denim—at once conspicuously and forever out of style. Scowling, and for long minutes more than ready to go, the man shifts his weight and watches the woman with the child. If he were a yeller, they would be hearing him curse this ineffectual woman and intractable child the whole way to Sunset Park. Their inability to accomplish something so simple as leave the

Bay Ridge McDonald's galls the man to no end. His agitation building, he clenches his fists into tight, calloused balls and pushes his athletic body up onto the toes of his white running shoes.

I can see clearly that this rancorous man is deeply disappointed that his life has come to this—a frumpy partner in an ill-fitting sweat suit and a badly behaved child fixated on a stuffed toy careening off an unmopped floor. These are the forces compelling him to piss away his Saturday afternoon lingering in a greasy McDonald's.

I watch the man *not* helping the woman as she tries clumsily to position the stroller to descend the stairs. He stands dead still, the exasperation coming off him like sweat.

I have seen this tension-suffused grimace before—twenty-five years in the past and several hundred miles west. Dozens of afternoons spent with my own small, sticky hands pushed deep into overcoat pockets, I've waited hour after hour in the lengthy, disordered lines of the unemployment office of an imploding Pennsylvania mill town with another very angry man seething above me.

Oh, yes. I know where this is heading.

I know the heart of this angry man. I know why he is wearing those horrible pants. I am sure that his car requires significant repairs every single goddamn month. I know for certain that tight-lipped forbearance of these privations is the only way he has left open for himself to show the hard love burning in him for this burdensome, cheerless family. That underneath the grinding bitterness and debilitating, unalloyed rage, it is his own inability to get somewhere in this world he blames for the predicament that is their daily life.

I want to offer this man-on-the-edge some words of encouragement. A few gentle words of congratulation for hanging on as long as he has without doing something drastic. I want to share the strength of my unencumbered and relatively sleek life, if only for a moment.

But I sit on the hard yellow bench at the bright orange table and finish my cheeseburger in silence, sadly unable to bridge the space between us. Halfway through my fries, I've had enough of this unpalatable fare and shove the meal—tray and all—into the trash can. I take the steps two at a time on the way down. I don't want to see what I know, sure as I know the face of my father, is going to happen next.

But it's no good. Sometimes fate must decide you will be a witness because I'm still fixed by the light at the crosswalk when they exit the restaurant. The woman starts forcing the stroller up the block, but there's some kind of disagreement of which I can't make out the details until she shouts, "Goddamn it, Bob! You made us forget our fucking drinks."

And that's when it happens. The man's eyes fix in an odd, malevolent way and before anyone can say so much as boo, the back of his hand has come up and gone back down again and the woman's face has jerked off to the side and her mouth is hanging open like she's been in a minor car accident.

Crossing the avenue, still unable to turn entirely away, I wonder if everything really bad that happens in the world can be traced to a series of moments like this one. Someone in a position to offer a kind word sits off to the side, silent and ineffectual.

But what really bothers me, the thing that worries me about all humanity, because I know this thing is lurking somewhere in your heart too, is that my shock at that actual moment, my grief at the way these people will continue their sad lives, even my shame for having done nothing in the face of a chance to do good, all of these are tinged—no, more than tinged—they are shot through with a dark pride that I was able to predict exactly what was going to happen, right down to the nearness of the event. This is what fills my head like poison as I walk away down 86th Street, to where my gleaming car waits in a covered lot.

A GRAPHICAL REPRESENTATION OF MY FIRST AND ONLY DATE WITH LAUREL WISENSTEIN, MARKETING COORDINATOR, EXPRESSED USING THE CHART FUNCTION OF MS POWERPOINT™

3:23PM, heart thumping in chest at her door

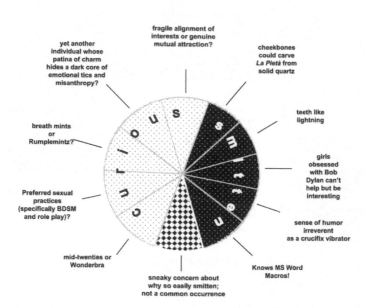

4:44PM, optimism flagging, Andy Warhol Museum

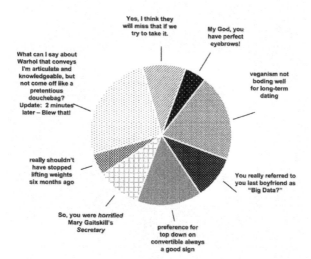

7:16PM, awash in apprehension, Sherry's Vegetarian Diner

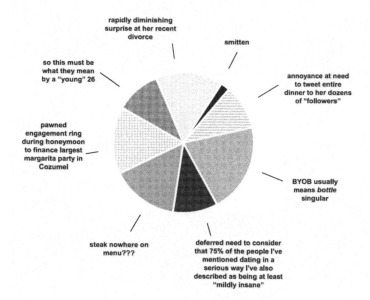

rapidly diminishing
surprise at her recent
divorce

smitten

so this must be
what they mean
by a "young" 26

annoyance at need
to tweet entire
dinner to her dozens
of "followers"

pawned
engagement ring
during honeymoon
to finance largest
margarita party in
Cozumel

BYOB usually
means *bottle*
singular

steak nowhere on
menu???

deferred need to consider
that 75% of the people I've
mentioned dating in a
serious way I've also
described as being at least
"mildly insane"

9:30PM, her driveway, fleeing to car

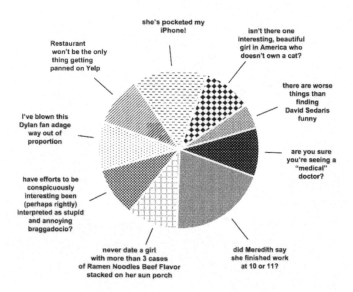

she's pocketed my
iPhone!

isn't there one
interesting, beautiful
girl in America who
doesn't own a cat?

Restaurant
won't be the only
thing getting
panned on Yelp

there are worse
things than
finding
David Sedaris
funny

I've blown this
Dylan fan adage
way out of
proportion

are you sure
you're seeing a
"medical"
doctor?

have efforts to be
conspicuously
interesting been
(perhaps rightly)
interpreted as stupid
and annoying
braggadocio?

never date a girl
with more than 3 cases
of Ramen Noodles Beef Flavor
stacked on her sun porch

did Meredith say
she finished work
at 10 or 11?

FABLES OF THE DECONSTRUCTION
#33: JAMESON ON POLISH HILL

DURING A 1978 RESEARCH trip to Pittsburgh's Polish Hill to interview working class males between the ages of twenty and forty-five about transitioning to service sector jobs, renowned cultural theorist Fredric Jameson finds himself in no small amount of trouble. Strolling the network of sidewalks off Carnegie Avenue, their macadam splintering like ice, Jameson has gotten himself involved in a heated discussion with Bruiser Stopko.

With twenty-one years in as a catcher in the wire mill at the Edgar Thomson Works—a well-paying, dangerous job performed in 130-degree heat and which, because of the sparks that light from the glowing ingots like bubbles from shaken champagne, demands a wool jumpsuit and padded gloves thick as law books—Bruiser has taken significant umbrage at Jameson's suggesting that sometime over the next five to ten years he will mostly likely be employed at minimum wage assembling gourmet sandwiches slathered with exotic mustard or spraying lawn chemicals on emerald green acre plots in front of oversized tract homes in the burgeoning Fox Chapel suburbs.

His Midwestern features ginning themselves into an excited frown, Jameson—grievously failing to anticipate the consequences of his assertion—throws perhaps too much in Bruiser's face his slackjaw academic's puzzlement at the millworker's inability to see the inevitable tumult and shift of the fast-coming future.

In the ensuing imbroglio, Bruiser, in the shadow of the crumbling frame houses that sprout from the hillside like weeds, gets off a quick combination of jabs and uppercuts which he caps off with a tremendous roundhouse right that knocks loose several of the cultural theorist's teeth. As Bruiser puts the finishing touches on his argument by twice bouncing Jameson's head off the roof of a nearby Buick, he finds it remarkable that the academic, for all his erudition, was unable to anticipate what he felt to be an embarrassingly well-telegraphed punch and failed to try to side-step it or even to duck.

Moral: No matter one's station, confronting unmanageable challenges thrusts keeping a weather eye to the foul blossoming future into the stark realm of near impossibility.

THAT'S A CODE 60, DISPATCH

YOU CAN'T, in all good conscience, say you're surprised to find Chuck Palahniuk shaking a naked, upside-down hooker in an attempt to rattle free a stolen gram of cocaine. You're also not shocked this is occurring at a book signing in a crowded mall outside Indianapolis. Nor are you astonished, not really, that he is shouting, "Give back my stash, you lowlife slit!"

What does shock the loose monkey shit right out of you is Chuck's not realizing that because the bitch is upside down, he's only shaking the coke *further into* her nose. Funny how sometimes conceptions of one's heroes can be simultaneously expanded and blown apart.

"Whom the Gods would destroy," you reflect. Or perhaps, the God within each of us must destroy the man or, more precisely, the humanity—so as to be revealed, the way cyanide leaching facilitates gold extraction.

Sure, you're also wondering if maybe you shouldn't have chased that pint of bonded whiskey with a quarter sheet of blotter acid. But topping all of this off is—of course—now's most salient question, "How the hell did Chuck talk you into holding this goddamn whore's other fucking leg? Chuck? Chuck? You there, buddy? Chuck?"

IN THE LAND BETWEEN THE VALLEY AND THE HILLS WHAT MEN SAID, THEY MEANT

— For Queue Gaynor

BEFORE THE BLUE was sailed by Columbus and his greedy, maritime ilk, before the men who followed him brought plagues, monotheism and gunpowder, there dwelt in the Piedmont a small band of itinerant tribesmen whose only wealth was the richness of their language.

That is not to say these men were simple or virtuous, for their greed for naming knew no bounds. Not only did each of their clear bright streams have a name, each ripple and waterfall possessed its own appellation, as did every gnat that circled the frothy swirls and each sharp-billed bird that feasted on the vast swarms of flittering black and each flat-billed bird that ignored the swarms and ate nothing but the variegated fish that you and I, in the poverty of our degenerate tongue, would call simply brook trout or brown trout or thick-bodied grass carp.

For these language-besotted tribesmen, the most crucial of their grueling tests in the passage to manhood was not the hunting of the panther, flush with danger, or the gathering of tubers, dull and numbing, but the rite of the naming competition.

To sit with the braves in the longhouse after the hunt and chew tobacco and spit juice into the fire and have the warm blood of a freshly slain hart splashed across his smooth face like dark water—that is to say, to achieve maturity and be deserving of respect—a boy first had to fashion a name for an object or person or feeling that shamed all others, one so superior in every respect that each member of the tribe forswore his own personal designation, until the boy-on-the cusp-of-manhood's name became the way the thing was known. Fashioning a designation was regarded a complex and exquisite task, demanding bold inventiveness tempered by maturity of mind and fierce accuracy of the senses, traits requisite to making a full contribution to the prosperity of the tribe.

Now, it happened that the naming trial of the son of the chief—a long looked to event, for succession hinged upon it—was in full swing on the cool, foggy morning the white men first came up from the sea, bristling in their hastily assembled plank canoes, paddles sliding through the water like knives and eyes agape for anything that could be transformed into money with a little shoddy effort. Adroit in the ways of camouflage, the tribesmen hid, secreting themselves behind boulders and straight-trunked firs, uncertain what to make of the albedonous strangers.

Hearts beating a slow, deliberate rhythm in their curving mahogany chests, the tribesmen watched as the whites beached their shiny boats and debarked into the incalculable swaths of dark forest. For months, with eyes narrowed and guts rife with suspicion, the tribesmen surveilled cautiously, scrutinizing the whites' tall tree chopping and their short tree chopping and their efforts to tear the land asunder with horse-drawn steel, as if they'd set out to disembowel the earth itself.

"Despoilers!" intoned one elder.

"Sons of bitches," spat another.

"They are like motherless children," suggested a square-faced squaw. "Unsure of their place in the world, they are desperate to make any kind of mark at all." She knew the kinds of things a woman learns caring for the four gangly sons of a sister who has slipped from a slick rock and drowned in one of the clear, fine-named rivers.

Skilled and clever in the art of remaining unseen, the tribe maintained its vigil, inventing and abandoning names for the white men and each of their transgressions as quickly as they could arrive at them. Even armed with their precise and powerful tongue, they struggled mightily to capture the white men's foul essence, for the depravity of their ways was unimaginable to the tribesmen.

Throughout this vigil the chief's son had remained silent in his hiding place, offering no suggested appellations for the white men or any of their misdeeds. He had said nothing about their wanton shooting of the game till only the rats were left, or their poisoning of the clear, well-named streams till they ran black, or the clear-cutting of the incalculable swaths of dark forest till the land was wretched and barren and sad in a way that broke the tribe's collective heart with every glance.

The elders watched and waited with tightening chests and shrinking bellies as more white men poured from larger ships and set quickly to the rapacious work of transforming the tip of the new continent into pounds and shillings. Knowing that in such straits the tribe would require a leader whose clarity of vision was commensurate with the stark challenge, they sought to inquire of the chief's son his thoughts on the correct name for the plundering strangers. But when they looked behind the scorched stump where he had been hiding, he offered them no words, no names, not so much as a syllable in the way of appellation.

This boy on the cusp of manhood had his hands splayed across his thin knees and on his lips sat only ashes. Pressed, the elders reminded him of the desperation of the times, how fate had presented the tribe with only bleak choices, a tragic portion.

"We can hold," they said, "to our language, rich and exact, perfecting it for our remaining short days in the ruined Piedmont or rise to embrace our final defeat in a short but glorious battle and thereby become something else altogether. Either way, we exchange our existence as a part of the shameful present for relegation to an honorable, if unheralded, past."

The son of the chief snorted and beckoned the elders closer, offering his own dark prescription. His eyes meeting only the blackened ground where a copse of vibrant elms and alders once thrived, he explained that the tribe must summon the courage to join with the white men. Assuming his place as chief, he announced the name he had decided for the perilous newcomers. "We must become less what we are," he told his fellow tribesmen, "and in so doing make them less what they are. Better all of us become a thing that is a small bit saved, than none be saved at all."

As their new chief tendered this sad counsel, the glum-faced tribesmen swallowed the broken bits of pride lodged in their mouths like tumors and nodded, acceding silently. But the sudden cessation of their constant murmur allowed the white men to finally hear the thud of their pounding hearts and the strident gurgle of their empty bellies and at long last discover the tribe's hiding place. Immediately, a fusillade of staccato cracks echoed through the smoky air of the Piedmont. The tribe looked down to find many of their brethren wounded and the chief's son perforated from scalp to sternum. Disconsolate beyond imagining, they packed up what remained of their words and disappeared back across the continent, naming only, in perpetuity, their retreat.

CLEANING HOUSE

KRISTIN VACUUMS our apartment for the sixth time today. She takes her sweet time inscribing elaborate hieroglyphics in the wheat-colored wall to wall. A word here, a phrase there. She is writing, she tells me curtly, the story of our marriage. This is the year after our honeymoon in Belize, she intones, making a series of quick swipes in front of the microfiber sectional. Moving toward the picture window, she languidly pushes her arm out and pulls it back in. We are now slow dancing, she says, to the Isley Brothers under the Saranac full moon the fall you got promoted. Minutes pass and she heads for the breakfront, her lines less controlled, thrusts taking on a grinding quality. You're spending a lot of time over in that corner, I say. Are you writing the summer I spent in Little Rock while you finished your securities license or those months sweltering in Boston during your Charles Schwab internship? Long past both, she laughs. This is the affair you had with that fat slut Babs Hamilton last Christmas when I was visiting my brother in Omaha. She repeatedly slaps the Hoover's carpet attachment into the baseboard. This is me discovering Babs Hamilton's bra right here behind the ficus. This is the afternoon at Sushi Café when I asked you if you'd stooped to screwing our friends' wives.

I do nothing when Kristin snatches the tenth anniversary TAG Heuer from my wrist, grinds it beneath her heel and vacuums it up off the tile floor of the kitchen. After she vacuums up my car keys, the remains of several credit cards and most of a necktie, I take a sip of coffee, assume we'll talk this out. But she vacuums up my flash drive, a top coat, my briefcase. I follow her through the apartment as the WindTunnel Anniversary Ultra™ with HEPA filter inhales a shelf of books, camping gear, fly rods, slalom skis and my vintage record collection. When Kristin has picked my closet clean, she tells me she is heading for the garage. I remind her I still have numerous payments to make on the Volvo. She shrugs, changes the bag, cuts me a look. The Volvo, she says, is only the beginning of her finding Babs Hamilton's daughter Linda's number on my phone last weekend.

4 WAYS OF LOOKING AT NASHVILLE

ONE

COMING UP HARD on the crumbling outskirts of a tiny, down-at-heel paper mill town in the hill country of rural Tennessee, Sharon had been molested repeatedly over a period of years by a father whose disappointment in life was so vast it took hold in terrible, unrelenting ways, warping him until he developed the regrettable ability to justify and act on impulses that under better circumstances he would have found despicable.

Lanky and formerly tomboyish, Sharon grew up doing her best to deny the all-encompassing destruction these horrible acts had visited on her gathering personality and pale, ruptured spirit —and wanting, more than anything, to learn to play the pedal steel.

She practiced dawn till dusk, possessed wholly by the conviction that if she could make those sweet, beautiful sounds well enough people would know she could be a bringer of untarnished loveliness. In the mildewing back bedroom of her daddy's clapboard shotgun, she wove and twined her fingers across the fret boards hour after hard hour, training them like fine-boned endurance athletes, building their memory, boosting their strength. Pushing at the pedals and plucking the taut steel strings, Sharon delved deep into the music, learning in time to draw low warbles and slow, descending twangs that could pull tears from a murderer's eyes.

As the seasons followed one another unvaryingly as an eight bar blues, Sharon became a veritable scholar of pedal steel, mastering the techniques of gaunt Depression Era virtuosos like Buddy Emmons and the Louvin Brothers—taciturn musicians who suffered humiliation and dilated hours toiling as sidemen for Roy Acuff and later Hank Williams.

Sharon even spent a summer in her late teens apprenticing as a stringer at the Sho-Bud Pedal Steel Guitar Company. Finally, when her dexterity was equal to any Louisville heart surgeon's and her knowledge of music was comprehensive as a college doyen's and the melodies she coaxed from the pedal steel were irreducibly her own, she headed for the glimmering lights of Nashville, rising up transformative and distant off the pine-dark gloom of the floodplain.

TWO

Its entrance sardined into the middle of a whitewashed row of historic buildings—many now converted to T-Shirt shops—stands brindled and squat as a bulldog one of the city's most enduring music venues. For decades so singular a launch pad to the firmament of country and western music that even the incon-stant shimmer of the front window's faulty neon sign is famed in song, the club easily ranks as one of the town's most storied, if not acoustically sound.

Centered in its smoke-filled, green room on a hickory stool, the club's bulge-gutted manager—avuncular, yet shifty—shirt-tail polishes his tear drop sunglasses as he reluctantly shitcans an aging fiddle player from Memphis who's shown up Tennessee two-step drunk one time too many.

"On the one hand, old son," the manager opines, "this is about discovering and sharing the truly awesome power of music." Pausing, he shifts his bulk on the stool and in a flush of showmanship strikes a match on the fly of his jeans to relight a cigar that has Fables of the Deconstruction 85 gone out. "But there's only so much dance card and a whole lotta mother-humpers *do* get off that Greyhound lookin' to hoof."

THREE

The after-party for the America's Farmers Benefit had ended only minutes ago, but most of our guests were already outside, standing on the cracked macadam of Woodrow Wilson pinching their valet tickets in the air like Mark over at the Polo Lounge had just brought them poop in their soup and they couldn't wait to yell at the manager.

Inside, Ronny sprawls on the sofa, Kentucky Bourbon sloshing in his glass and his feet tucked up under him like a dog in trouble. The Altman movie is long over and the screen shows nothing but snow and he hasn't even turned the volume the whole way down. Maybe because his ears are ruined from the last tour or maybe because he just doesn't give a shit.

"A goddamn hick is all I'll ever be to these assholes, Sharon," he says, dismissing with a sloppy gesture the dozens of rich folks that come over after the fundraiser to smirk at *Nashville*.

Ronny's eyes are fixed on the guest house of our neighbor, a newscaster who, I'm told, never comes to Laurel Canyon anymore. The hokum in his voice thick as Karo, as buttermilk, thick as the shame used to be when we first moved out here, Ronny harangues me again about his growing up country, the lack of shoes, the lack of culture, the just plain lack.

"I come up country too," I tell him, but he's not listening.

"Music was the only thing kept me from longhaulin' goddamn hogs Chattanooga to Memphis like my pa," he says. "Man was never home a full week from the time I was nine."

"I know, baby," I say. I try to keep clear of starting in thinking about my own pa, what he's done and where he is now.

"Maybe I am just a hick," Ronny says, ignoring me. "I mean Monty hadn't a fired Mothball Wilson for showin' up too drunk to fiddle four nights outta six, I might be gear jamming a semi full a goddamn razorbacks this very minute."

As self-pity isn't an attractive quality for anybody and even less so for a man who's sold out whole arenas worth of tickets at forty dollars a head, I just keep quiet till Ronny can pivot all that energy into puffing himself back up, which, truth told, never takes too god awful long.

"Course if I am a hick, it just means these swishy assholes come out tonight to kiss the ass of the king of hick music. Shit, they probably can't even stand what I play." "Music means a lot to all kinds a folks," I say, my hands full of ashtrays that are either half-full or half-empty. I'm thinking about the money raised tonight, how it will help stall off the foreclosures.

"What the shit would you know about it?" Ronny snarls, bouncing off the sofa into the middle of the room like it's center stage. "Even when you was playin' P steel for me back in Nashville, music was never nothing more than a damn hobby for you."

FOUR

Pushing the cart down the aisle on D block I watch it pick up the row of shadows where the bars block out the weak sunlight blinking through the window. The wheels on the cart squeak and it's on my last nerve and none of the other rapists probably want to read back issues of the *Christian Science Monitor* anyway, but I keep asking.

"Y'all boys want some reading materials?" I ask them. Little else passes between my lips these days.

What I call The Silence started the night my daughter's band opened for Travis Tritt down Nashville. She'd asked me not to come, but I was rolling up the I-40 jazzed on poppers in a pickup I'd owned two grand in repairs too long. Roy Acuff was on the radio singing, "Great Speckled Bird," and crossing the county line sure as I'm in this place now, I heard Jesus talking to me through the AM radio.

"Cyrus McIlroy," the Lord was saying over the twang. "I know the poison in your heart."

I double clutched and shifted, but even gunnin' up to ninety I couldn't outrun the Lord. My sins were mortal and legion, He said over the rattle of the muffler and the bang of the push rods. My sins were grievous, an abomination, a stink in the nostrils of the most high. I was a twitch-mouthed, crooked-walking Sodom, a pickup-drivin' Gomorrah. Compassed by travail, I was fast on the brimstone expressway to damnation.

I slid over onto the rutted shoulder of the Interstate and that's when the offer come down. There was hope for me yet. The fix was not all the way in. I could escape the reaping whirl-wind, the voice said. There was a way.

I drove direct to the Charlotte Pike Police Station. I told them doubtless and quiet the way I destroyed my little girl from the inside out. I told them about the creak of the bedsprings and smell of talc sweet as damnation. I told them sloe-eyed pigs they should lock me up until Jesus comes back.

The other men here say the lights cherrytopping the new skyscrapers in town shimmer off the cloud banks in bad weather at night, but I won't look. In this place my eyes stay fixed on the beast in the mirror, searching the splinters of what's broken up inside for clues back to being a man. There are even moments that I forget I'm a monster.

But let me be plain now: I know this isn't enough, for the things I've done allow no *enough* and the dark paths I've followed aren't ones from which a man returns a man. So, no mistake, I'm easy with this. Suffering and quiet excision are better than I deserve and the last, best sad offering I can make to deliver my little girl's heart a shard closer to peace.

SCALENE

THE BABY still isn't sleeping, so my mom jerks the Toyota onto the causeway for another lap, ignoring the fact that I have a test in Fundamentals of Geometry first thing tomorrow morning. She's humming along with the radio and won't look over to see me clenching my teeth or flaring my nostrils or glaring out the tinted window like I'm about to pull a *Carrie* on every living thing in the state of Mississippi from the millshacks to the cane-breaks to this tar-shining highway that called her last boyfriend down to New Orleans in his leveraged semi after he knocked her up, saddling us with this squalling bundle of white.

ENTRY 5,714

from *The Whiskey Dictionary*

PET: (proper noun) Nickname of Andy Capp's wife which some may—after a slight struggle—remember from the Sunday Funnies read over cups of after-church coffee at grandmother's frame house during the hour of calm before the arrival of the uncle who gets boisterous after drinking and who had *always* been drinking heavily on Sunday mornings before visiting, perhaps because he felt it imperative to put a fiery wall of liquor between his mind and the judgments of his family about the mess he's made (and continues to make) of his life—a conclusion about the compartmentalizing power of alcohol you will come to embrace and reject on and off over the years about things like your own family (extended and nuclear), more jobs than you can count, weeknight television, traffic, meals, skiing, artwork, all the things, basically, experienced when you're awake, including your own wife, whose nickname, incidentally, is Sugar.

WHAT WE DON'T TALK ABOUT WHEN WE TALK ABOUT YOUR COUSIN WHO'S IN PRISON

TOPPING our household's list of conversation topics surely isn't class difference—which is why you can sit here at the butcher block table in our fancy Westwood condo plucking Sugar in the Raw packets from a Limoges sugar caddy your mother found antiquing somewhere north of Saratoga and hold forth on the tragedy of the decaying teeth of your crackhead cousin which, along with the rest of him, are deservedly rotting in some South Carolina jail for holding up two Charleston liquor stores on the same day, and what we will *never* discuss is the soggy afternoon you finally ventured to my grandmother's ramshackle house where—over his mispronunciation of "Merlot" when offering a glass of wine—you condescended blatantly to Chick, the cousin of *mine* with the overbite who served two tours as a combat sergeant in Iraq and now works double shifts searching fat women trying to smuggle weed into a minimum security prison when he's not rehabbing houses outside of Gary, but in my family that's par for the course or maybe even a birdie, not that we use golf metaphors, as outside of badminton or ornithology my father wouldn't know a birdie from a hole in the wall, of which he's got plenty due to his temper and the drinking. So tell me again about how your convict cousin is such a good kid even though he was tossed out of Bowdoin for statutory rape and cheating off the scholarship boys on two terms' worth of physics exams.

*

So, *fine*, let's talk about class *difference*, Richard. Like how little difference the acting classes that prevent you from holding a full time job have made in the number of roles you've gotten this year and yeah, I know, it's really cool that you got a speaking part on *True Detective* and I know it's a hot show and that HBO is a great network and I *don't* mean to diminish your accomplishments, but how dare you come on like that about *our* condo when I'm the one who's not going on vacation again this year because I'm paying your half of the outlandish maintenance fees and if I remember right it was you who just had to live in goddamned Westwood in the first place which means I spend every morning stuck in traffic for an hour since they started construction on Santa Monica Boulevard and just so we're fucking straight here *Richard*, before you start in on my *family* it might not kill you to keep in mind that my dad's putting me through medical school at Hopkins is the only reason I'm not in debt up to my eyes and can afford to be *seriously romantically involved* with a guy who's obviously unlikely to ever pay his share of our bills and not choke on my own wholesale resentment of it every single, goddamn minute of the livelong day, *Richard*.

HE NEEDS YOUR HELP!

AT THE END of my non-biodegradable rope with various quarters' distaste for my shaky consumer ethics, I hereby vow to scrub my act cleaner than the exhaust from a fuel cell commuter plane —and I'm turning to you, esteemed readers of this high-quality web publication, for support. When it comes to making morally sound product choices, you, dear reader, can "do good" by helping me do better.

Let's start with essentials. Food, for instance. Fed up with Damian contributing to the destruction of what little is left of the Argentinean pampas through his consumption of hormone-laden burger chain beef? For only $35.00 a month, you can ensure that Damian only chows down on free-range, grass finished meats raised by gentlemen farmers in picturesque, rural Vermont.

Not a carnivore? A paltry $20.00 guarantees Damian's eschewing of vegetables grown with conventional oil-based fertilizers in favor of eco-friendly organics. Too rich for your blood? A lousy $10.00 a month can ensure Damian purchases only Fair Trade coffee. No more abetting the ripping off of exploited Colombian coffee-picking teens for Damian.

Still beyond your means? Even the most parsimonious or

skint can contribute. A PayPal donation of just $12.00 every three months and you can rest assured that Damian's short, dark hair will be washed only with cruelty-free organic shampoo and not the shit from the dollar store he's been buying.

Damian's needs also include energy efficient appliances. His thirteen-year-old refrigerator in particular is hogging much more than its share of power from the East Coast's fragile, outdated grid. While Damian would consider trading up to gently-used models, the improvements garnered through such half-measures would be incremental at best. True, state-of-the-art ethics really require that Damian enjoys the energy savings of new durable goods. For example, the LG 27 cubic foot counter depth French door with InstaView™.

A special additional appeal: For years now—more than he's willing to admit, really—Damian has been listening to a publicly supported radio station for several hours daily without forking over one dime toward membership. Contributions, in this limited circumstance, should be mailed (in Damian's name, of course) *directly* to Pittsburgh's WQED.

While Damian's newly discovered ethics are, in fact, real, there is a rumor his electric bill is also overdue. Why force Damian to flirt with temptation when his new ethics of consumption are small, fragile things that could easily crumple in a strong fiscal wind?

And for the folks out there truly committed to correcting the inequities on Damian's karmic balance sheet, there exists a special one-time giving opportunity: a donation of a mere $22,459 would allow Damian to trade in his aging, fossil fuel guzzling Nissan Pathfinder on a new hybrid. Tell me there isn't one person out there who wants to see Damian stop jamming his thick, carbon-stained fingers straight into the cornflower blue eyes of Mother Earth and start getting forty-eight ecologically sound miles per electricity-supplemented gallon.

Remember, without the efforts of good people like you, it

would be all too easy for Damian, victim of rampant self-interest that he is, to backslide into the morass of his selfish and unsustainable ways. So, reach for those checkbooks and say it with me now: "Only *we* can help Damian help himself!"

OOOOPS!

A FILCHED bottle of red wine slips from under Ed's night watchman windbreaker as he steals from the firm's kitchen toward the elevator, exploding in a streaky, purple Jackson Pollock across the freshly-polished marble floor and "fuck!" now he's going to be kissing the ass of the goddamn janitor or yet another good job goodbye.

FABLE OF THE DECONSTRUCTION #43: BORN UNDER A BAD SIGNIFIER: JIM FROM CRITICAL THEORY 2012

THE CLOCKS HAVE BEEN STUCK at three for days and while some people blamed the aliens who hover above Mellon Arena in their shimmering silver ship, Jim is pretty sure he's responsible. He's vowed to cease his chronic navel gazing and scale way back on his unrelenting what-if-ery, but even now catches himself wondering: "If only I'd stopped ruminating on all my past mistakes sooner, this might never have happened."

ROBBERY BY THE NUMBERS

THE SEDAN IS ATLANTA BLUE, stolen and accelerating at a rate of 52 meters/second. The driver, a recently fired network engineer with $73,000 of unpayable student loan debt and an IQ of 108, can't believe it has come to this. Twenty-seven inches long, the sleeping child in the back seat has been the subject of numerous conversations in the last 18 months involving lawyers billing between $175 and $250 per hour. The car thief (née network engineer; identity is fluid), whose mortgage payments outstrip his unemployment benefits by $375 per month, doesn't know the child is there, but overwhelmed by circumstance and adrenaline he might not behave differently. On the sidewalk, three police officers in blue polyester and one security guard earning $11.00 per hour assume lateral stances. Semi-automatic .45 caliber handguns discharge. A flurry of ACP 230 grain slugs blister the air a few lucky feet above the curved roofline. No one fires a second shot once the frantic parents start shouting about the BABY!

Tucked into a thirty cubic inch North Face backpack centered on the passenger's seat, twelve thousand dollars in small bills represents the driver's diminishing future. The dye pack waiting to explode underneath represents the interest of the state. The parents, hyperventilating as the car squeals onto the service road, represent nothing. They are simply two flawed people who might not get divorced if the man can stop drinking rye whiskey, the woman can stop looking for something better to come along, the baby doesn't awaken and start squalling loudly, causing the thief, already panicked, to swivel his head 130 degrees in surprise and crash head on into the police van speeding to answer the urgent radio call of the first officer to stop shooting.

LISTING

VISITING after karaoke night at Shaunessy's, I find my mother loaded in the living room. Two used fentanyl patches sit on a DVD case on the coffee table. Foil-lined bags lie crumpled on the floor next to the sofa. She stares at season two of *Weeds*. Headphone cables run from her ears to my brother's laptop.

"Karen," she asks me. "Do you think I look like Mary Louise Parker?" She is sipping jug wine from a coffee mug.

There are three things I want her to be healthy enough to hear:

1. You don't look a damn thing like Mary Louise Parker.
2. You'd feel a lot better if you stopped feeling sorry for yourself and act more like the 100 pound ball of threat who chased the vice principal with a TASER the afternoon he paddled my sister.
3. You were the one who swore you'd never let yourself be defined by a label like "cancer patient."

At the very goddamned least I want her to be ferociously

angry that I've been driving or to tell me to stop thinking of myself—that she's the one who's dying. "Nah," I say, finally, deciding I've got to start somewhere. "Mary Louise Parker—that woman has a much better ass."

LIGHT OF THE WORLD

ONCE UPON A TIME, there was a large corrugated metal building, low and squat, filthy with coal dust and vast as ten thousand football stadiums. The people who lived there called it The World. The sky above The World had been thick with black and gray smoke for so long no one could remember there were stars and the existence of the sun was a matter only of half-hearted conjecture.

The tight-lipped, put-upon people who lived in The World grumbled their way through sad lives—griping from dirty cradle to filthy grave as their days followed one another like an endless chain of bleak tasks that rightfully should have been assigned to someone else.

*

The language of The World had a dozen words for soot and more than a hundred for failure. In the language of The World every word secretly meant shame and the closest thing there was to an expression of victory was saying "I don't care." The word for "hello" meant scarcity. Even the word for "beautiful" also meant temporary and the word for "ambition" meant escape. It also meant laughable and hopeless.

*

The people of The World earned their daily bread by selling a carefully measured portion of their hearts—each week a line was formed and the bits weighed on a special scale by a grim foreman. Luxuries could only be procured, if at all, through the bartering of dreams or the foregoing of children.

*

After spending their days digging heavy black stones from tunnels deep in the earth or carting the stones by railcars the color of soot to capacious blast furnaces or feeding the black stones into the furnaces, The World's people came home to two-room wood frame houses that smelled of sour cabbage and coal dust and anger sometimes kept in check.

The World's people had done these things for as long as there had been tunnels in the earth or railroad cars the color of soot or capacious blast furnaces or even people in The World, and no one could imagine a time when this life—one that everyone knew was stunted and poor and shallow and in which bearing this knowledge more quietly than anyone else was called "character"—would not be the way of things.

*

Year after year everything in The World got slowly worse unless it got worse fast.

Either there were too many black stones or not enough or the wood frame houses' decay accelerated catastrophically or the people were increasingly slighted on the sale of the hearts by the foreman's finger on the tare.

*

Many of The World's people believed it was held together by a secret—the kind of secret that everyone knows but pretends they don't. The secret was this: It was not the heavy black stones shipped on railcars the color of soot, but their very own bright-burning souls combusting in the capacious blast furnaces that kept them alight.

*

One day, word came in a blinding flash from outside The World that the capacious blast furnaces would be extinguished, their doors shuttered and the locomotives the color of soot would run no more. Stricken, the people of The World offered their still-beating hearts as fuel for the capacious blast furnaces, but were told the time of burning the blast furnaces was over and anyway, their crummy hearts were used-up.

Hearing this, the people of The World cleaved into camps. The first wanted to set the capacious blast furnaces aflame and derail the locomotives the color of soot and collapse for good the entrances to the holes in the earth where the heavy black stones were mined. The second wanted to supplicate themselves further, drowning like kittens in a bathtub what little remained of their dreams, in an attempt to win over those claiming the time of the blast furnaces was finished.

The second group was larger, but the first more committed and both sides were really only asking "What shall become of us?" and neither accomplished anything much as liens were fixed to the two-room wood frame houses and the lining up for the sale of hearts was scaled back to every other week.

*

The World's children watched as parents were bent and

broken and crushed under the weight of the shame and the inability to do anything in the face of the shuttering of the blast furnaces and the closing of the holes in the earth. And while in shoddily built schools the children had learned Don't Stand Out Unless You're Unassailably Strong and Power is Another Thing You'll Never Possess—at home in the two-room wood frame houses that smelled of sour cabbage and defeat and anger now rarely kept in check, mostly they learned No Matter How Meager Your Dreams Are, They Can Be Taken Away.

And as the two-room wood frame houses that smelled increasingly of inactivity and No Food At All and anger boiling assiduously over *were* taken away, from outside The World came offers of help.

*

Arriving in shiny, aerodynamic cars, the helpers made the people of The World line up for small amounts of Food That No One Else Wanted and stand for days at a time waiting to have tiny holes punched in yellow rectangular cards in exchange for amounts of money that the people of The World invariably described as Nowhere Near Enough to save the two-room wood frame houses. And while they stood in the lines for rotting food and they waited days at a time to have the tiny holes punched in their yellow rectangular cards, the people of The World understood that they were even more worthless than they had suspected as they were told they ought to feel grateful.

*

This standing in line for Food That No One Else Wanted and waiting days at a time for the tiny holes to be punched in the yellow rectangular cards went on until the people in the shiny cars became bored with helping the people of The World and with narrowed eyes, and teeth straightened and white as paper, asked "Can't these idiots do anything to help themselves?" Then they slipped back into the shiny, aerodynamic cars and drove away very fast seeking to spend their finite energy someplace closer to the ocean where the people were urbane and optimistic and not small-minded or ruined in any way at all.

*

"Wait! Wait!" called the people of The World. "What about our secret? What about our bright-burning souls molten and alight for so long in the furnaces?"

"Your secret?" asked the helpers. "Your secret is a lie. Your souls were not worth burning. And if maybe some of them did burn in the furnaces? So what? Even if your grimy souls did give off some light, they are long used up and ashen and besides, it wasn't very good light anyway."

*

Left alone, one by one or in groups, the people of The World came to the blackened doors of the capacious blast furnaces even though they suspected it would do no good. Using cooled pieces of metal they tried to fish what remained of their precious bright-burning souls from the hulking, empty furnaces, but little remained and nothing worth taking.

Later, when the people of The World died, their spent lungs the color of the railcars the color of soot, they were buried in narrow graves which no one came to visit and everyone forgot as quickly as they could. And no one told the story of The Light of The World because everyone who was from that place was either ashamed of coming from there or broken by leaving.

PROXY

IT'S three o'clock in the morning after their first Oscar party in the new place and Kevin Flaherty is pumping into his wife like there's no tomorrow. Shoving her tiny wrists deep into the hypoallergenic pillow, Kevin brings all of his 225 pounds to bear as he pushes into her. His eyes shut tight, Kevin's doing his best to keep hold of a mental picture of Sandy, one of his wife's younger coworkers, a plump girl with bad skin who stumbled into the party mid-Billy Crystal monologue clutching a well dented bottle of Tanqueray Ten.

Puddled between Kevin and his wife at the gathering's epicenter, Sandy kept explaining that she wasn't really a slut, she was just drunk. She said this every time Kevin's wife pushed her left hand away from its assiduous march up Kevin's inner thigh.

As Kevin pushes himself into the tightness of his wife, he focuses on the sensory details of an exchange with her coworker an hour earlier. After following him through the narrow apartment to the subway-tiled bathroom, Sandy thrust her way in and flung her arms around his neck, pressed her heavy breasts into his chest.

"I'll be a good girl for you," she told him.

Digging her pudgy fingers into Kevin's buttocks, Sandy

ushed her tongue into his mouth. He kissed her back for a minute before stepping away.

"Wait," he told her. "I'll drive you home."

But Sandy wasn't driven home by Kevin or anyone else. After a second trip to the bathroom during which she lifted her shirt and Kevin fondled her breasts through her bra, Sandy passed out on their Castro convertible with her mouth open.

Kevin suspects his wife knows what he's thinking about, knows who he's imagining he's on top of, but she's not saying anything. Unable to get the next morning off from the travel agency, Cheryl probably wants him to hurry and finish so she can get some sleep before a hectic morning fielding calls from vacationers rearranging trips due to the flu outbreak.

The evening's incident with Sandy is the first time anything like this has happened to Kevin in six years of marriage. He's curious if his losing thirty pounds over the last five months means that these kinds of opportunities will become a regular part of his life. He's also curious about what would have happened if he had indeed driven Sandy home. Would he have actually gone ahead with it? Would he have at least let her unzip his fly and take him into her mouth at some anonymous exit off the Long Island Expressway?

Kevin knows that after he comes inside his wife, he'll be glad he wasn't tested. But for this sweaty, elated second—good god!—he can feel his hand lost in that short, dark hair and smell the gin fresh on her breath, juniper sweet as freedom.

DOWN ALONG THE CONDADO

BY THE TIME they got to the tall, white hotel on the ritzy edge of the Condado, Mark and Bette knew the best days of their relationship were behind them. This sad knowledge didn't stop them from strolling the white sand beaches, thin fingers interlocked or gazing out across the blue Caribbean at the ketches sliding across the flat water like elaborate sleds carving glass.

They maintained their banter—riffing on the waiter's solicitude and polished brass manner—as they wolfed down *huevos rancheros* at Monday's Welcome to the Islands Breakfast. Amidst the lush foliage of Tuesday's Spice Caye Nature Walk, their repartee never slackened, having its way with the fleet-footed lizards and wily marmosets and giant parrots the color of blood.

Teeth gritted, Mark still fetched Bette's Bellinis from the wild-haired bar man at the Tiki Shack and grudgingly nudged her for hints as he bumbled his way through the Tuesday crossword. Bette, for her part, cooed sweet nothings, kneading Hawaiian Tropic into Mark's broad, smooth-muscled shoulders —all the while contemplating garroting him with the granny strap of his Oakleys or liberally flavoring his Mai Tai with nail polish remover.

By midweek, they could hardly help but refer to each other

as Darling and Sweetheart, pedestrian sobriquets they imagined would have certainly never crossed their adroit, urbane minds before things had so obviously gone to sixes and sevens. Spooning in a wide hammock stretched between two coconut palms, they nuzzled, murmuring their newfound endearments—minds busily calculating the likelihood of slipping off to the international airport unseen.

The weekend was worse. They couldn't even get through a glass of fume blanc without twining their toned arms and sipping from each other's flutes, clandestinely speculating if the thin crystal was robust enough for a meaningful stabbing. By Saturday's Eco-Tour Day Trip to Bahía Mosquito, their compulsion to moon and smile at each other from the skiff's opposite gunwales trailed only narrowly behind their burgeoning need to fling the other vestless from the narrow boat into the unvarying drift of the Gulf Stream.

By the time Sunday's red snapper was centered on the dinner linen, things had gotten to the point where Mark felt he must speak up, must finally say something that would change things irrevocably, else he would go stark raving.

Eyes fixed on an empty spot of tablecloth between the shrimp and summer corn bisque and lobster empanadas, Mark steeled himself. After a few false starts, he finally managed to unburden himself.

When the waiter, previously the object of such humor, presented, unordered, a blazing Bananas Foster, not a smile was cracked. Solemnity ruled the small rectangular table like a sultan his harem as Mark waited for Bette to speak.

"Of course," Bette said. "Of course."

Her bottom lip edged into the shape of a half moon, Bette felt every imaginable future suffused with passion and joy recede forever in a ruinous blur of veiled acrimony and routine.

"Absolutely," she said. "I will marry you."

SEVEN AGAINST TONY

First off, the title. Appropriated from Aeschylus's late period static tragedy, *Seven Against Thebes,* (and sent quickly down-market) the *Seven* in this instance reference the malevolent forces arrayed against, not a 4th century B.C. attic city state, but a down-at-the-heel 21st century protagonist whose Anthony—cocksure with regal implication, has been shortened, diminished, chopped, if you will—to the juvenile and informal, Tony. It should also be made clear that the Tony in question is solely the product of the author's imagination and is in no way intended as a portrayal—even if those in the know may spot the odd similarity— of his addled, irresponsible cousin of the same name.

Perfunctories presently dispensed, we may formally begin ordering the powers arrayed against our besieged central character. First and foremost when enumerating his antagonists, we must name Tony, himself. Of course seeing any man as his most potent enemy is no mighty piece of perspicacity, and in this case the exercise could be considered downright facile, given the way our boy is crumpled against the lime green living room wall, Krispy Kreme-augmented ass plumb to the floor he never got around to refinishing, unpaid bills fanned like a losing poker hand on a

COMMENT: If it does ring a bell and are complimenting yourself (somewhat smugly, I'd imagine) on your sterling erudition and impressive recall, it's likely that both are the result of good genetics and/or well-intentioned, middle to upper-middle class parents sending you to a solid and pricey liberal arts college, neither of which can you take any meaningful degree of credit for. Not really.

COMMENT: Yes, this is the blacksheep cousin who did six months in county for passing a bad check to pay for the installation of ceramic composite brake pads on an about-to-be-repossessed Z-28 Camaro.

COMMENT: Please note our shared class bias here—were Tony's ass augmented by freshly baked gluten-free baguettes topped with sun-dried tomatoes and oven-softened gruyere, would we be so harsh in our judgment?

nearby table, and synapses paralyzed by self-pity since long before his estranged wife Shannon said, "Sayonara, Ass Hat!" and moved back in with her mother months ago—before the oak leaves flush with tannin killed the grass or the bank agent started up with the envelopes color-coded to imply various degrees of urgency or the package store changed its weekly order from United Importers to keep pace with Tony's seemingly unquenchable thirst for VAT 69 Scotch whiskey, a measure of which currently stains the t-shirt he's been wearing for the last two days in a pattern that looks remarkably like a map of Umbria.

Second (or first, were our slobbering protagonist the one charged with the ordering) would be the aforementioned Shannon, a diner waitress whose ungovernable passion for embezzlement is exceeded only by her irascibility and chronic need to blame others for her shortcomings and bad choices, of which her acceptance of a drunken marriage proposal in a trash-strewn hallway from such an obvious loser as Tony is only the most recent life-changing example.

Tied for third and fourth place as contributors to Tony's downfall—possibly second and "Not a Factor" were his VA-appointed psychiatrist to interrupt his annual birdwatching trip to the white sand beaches of Ambergris Caye, Belize to weigh in—are the violent, dyspeptic father from whom Tony inherited his tendency to respond to stress by alternately shutting down emotionally or succumbing utterly to thrill seeking behavior like check kiting or voluble street arguments begging to escalate into physical violence

AND the PTSD acquired in the ill-conceived Middle East incursion that plucked Tony from his uneventful life as a competent short order cook and serviceable, if uninspired, national guardsman and thrust him into the oven-hot ethnic minefield of Dyalla Province where he witnessed, among other atrocities, a thirty-year-old woman simulate a late-stage pregnancy by strapping a bulky belt of improvised explosives around her waist and detonate herself in the serpentine line of a Shia-owned falafel stand, painting the high, dun-colored sandstone walls of the nearest building horror movie red with the draped intestines of two school-age children.

Not that there need be further powers challenging Tony for ownership of the series of loose ends he's come to regard as his life, but full understanding of his predicament demands at least a cursory mention of Duquesne Light, which has relentlessly confused him with another Tony of the Same Last Name — one whom prior to fleeing the state for income tax evasion ran up $19,000 of unpaid electric bills in various condominiums and frame houses throughout Allegheny County thus causing constant, if temporary, interruptions of electrical service for our Tony, one which is the most obvious, but not the most meaningful reason Tony is sitting in the dark in his crumbling duplex listening to the Steelers vs. Patriots on Sunday Night Football via the crackling squawk of a battery-operated transistor radio.

Sixth—and although to most observers he might seem awfully remote to be so intimately involved with Tony's fate—is none other than Tom-Fucking-Brady who, after having been listed as questionable all damn week and dutifully sitting out the first three quarters, has entered the game after his backup left with a broken collar bone and just completed a forty-yard pass to wide receiver Danny Amendola, setting up a potentially game-winning field goal with only 26 seconds to play.

Penultimately, and unquestionably the most immediate threat to Tony's well-being, is Bruiser Stopko, a collector for Tony's bookie, and by far the most important reason Tony has tuned into the game in the perilous dark. Bruiser currently circles Tony's block in his blue F-150 pickup smoking a cigarillo and waiting for the late season game to end. Behind the truck's heated leather passenger's seat lurks like a carcinoma the 34-inch, 48-ounce Louisville Slugger that Bruiser will employ to beat Tony within an inch of his life if Stephen Gostkowski successfully kicks the 42-yard field goal and as the sportscasters say, puts the Patriots "up for good."

The final force that must be thrown on the scales (although whether it belongs on the side of good or ill remains uncertain) is the unlicensed Armstrong County gun dealer who, in his low level greed and fanatical belief in the Second Amendment, allowed Tony to bypass the mandatory mental health background

COMMENT: A pronounced departure here from the Greeks' preferred dramatic structure, a central feature of which demanded an exact sense of closure—so necessary to their aesthetic that the dramatic tension in many plays resolved through a *deus ex machina*, literally "god from a machine." Instead we find ourselves knee deep in the post-modernist notion of ambiguity, which suggests the position of the onlooker is itself so unfixed as to preclude attaching an unalterable meaning to any specific outcome.

COMMENT: While Bruiser doesn't *not* enjoy his new line of work, sometimes when he drives past the Edgar Thomson Works, he pines for his old job on the labor gang in the long shuttered wire mill. Though dangerous and demanding, the gig never forced him to consider the unpleasantness of a full-on confrontation with his claustrophobia were he saddled with a twenty month stretch in the Allegheny County Jail for simple assault. That said, Bruiser does enjoy getting to spend more time with his family, as he now gets to more or less set his own hours.

check in his quest to procure a gray market .22 caliber semi-automatic pistol with which he plans to commit suicide if he loses his substantial double or nothing bet on the Steelers defeating the Patriots, but which in the heat of the moment Tony may just fire to defend himself against a crushing blow from Bruiser Stopko's hard-swung bat and so again infuse his life with meaning, defining it above all else as something for which he has fought valiantly in the face of great danger and heroically won.

COMMENT: Which, after the accident involving the indoor rocket propelled grenade launch earned him an unceremonious Section 8 and rotation Stateside, Tony would have certainly and spectacularly failed.

###

VICTORY

—for Dominic Dunne

ONCE UPON A TIME, an unsuccessful writer followed well-known editors everywhere. Elevators. Taxi cabs. Even to the bathroom. Finally, after weeks of careful planning, the unsuccessful writer cornered his quarry one afternoon in the stairwell of a parking garage on Lexington Avenue.

"What do you want from us?" the exasperated editor asked, eager to put an end to the unsuccessful writer's aggravating pursuit.

"I want to be successful," said the unsuccessful writer.

"That's easy," the editor replied. "Just tell everyone what they want to hear." For many years, the writer did just this. Told the old it was not so bad to be old. Told the poor they were privy to raw pleasures the rich would never experience. Told the rich they bore no guilt for the reckless way they lived their lives and that they were hard lives, too, for all their entitlement and ease. "Hard. Hard. Hard," the writer wrote again and again. "The lives of the rich are hard."

This made the unsuccessful writer very successful. He bought a car that rode as if on rails. A cantilevered house with a view of Lake Hollywood. Women with eyes the color of seawater carried his typewriter wherever he went. And he only read books that told him how hard successful writers struggled, constantly working at the edge of their ability to figure out what people wanted to hear.

THE MARGARITA TRUCE OF SOUTH 5TH STREET

I DON'T COMPLAIN when my mother drinks. I don't say a solitary word the Friday nights she comes home from the Roundup, lists through the dining room, tequila splashed across her rayon skirt, purse full of scratch-offs and millwrights' phone numbers. I just let her carom into the bathroom, turn on the spigot, lower her head and knee the door shut. I don't even give her shit Saturday mornings when all she can eat are Tums and generic aspirin.

Since the Army's visit about my dad, she's stopped asking me questions too. Math, science, the money missing from her purse. Nothing about the diet pills or four tiny x's incised on the inside of my left thigh under my stocking—one for each boy. We both know the calm can't last forever. Inside us hurricanes turn, gather unfathomable strength. But for just now, this trapeze silence—the universe's tiny benison.

BREAKFAST AT BETHANY'S

YOU ARE AT BETHANY'S. Again.

You have promised yourself, over and over, that you would not end up here. In the morning. Like this.

Fourteen hours, and several dozen drinks ago, you thought the two of you looked like an advertisement for cool, hetero-sexual Los Angeles. Staring at Bethany now, with her rat's nest and raccoon eyes, and at your own shaking hand, you decide this is no longer the case. In the hyper-white light in the kitchen of Bethany's tiny Studio City apartment, you decide the only thing the two of you could possibly be used to advertise at this point is the Betty Ford Center.

You have been leaving messages on the answering machine of a friend who's out of town in a vague attempt to document the summer. In June, these messages often began, "Guess whose bed I woke up in this morning?" In July, this progressed to, "Guess whose floor I woke up *on* this morning?" If you had to leave a phone message concerning the events of last night, it would run something along the lines of, "Guess which exit on the Santa Monica Freeway we took before passing out on the side of the road for three hours? Don't worry, your guess is as good as mine."

Bethany is lighting a cigarette from a burner on the stove.

Lighting cigarettes, she has told you, is the only reason she hasn't had the gas turned off. She doesn't cook, ever. And she can't keep her shit together long enough to depend on being able to find a lighter. Bethany takes a kind of bizarre pride in facts like this. This is typical of the people with whom you have been spending your summer.

Breakfast will consist of too strong Kenya AA, cigarettes, and possibly an argument. Bethany and you seem to argue a lot, in the way that people who have been married for a long time argue. Which is ridiculous. You have only known each other for three months.

"Hey," Bethany says, "Whatcha thinkin' about?"

You consider responding with the old Andrew Dice Clay joke, "If I wanted you to know, I'd be talking." You decide this may not be the most rewarding salvo in your efforts to achieve domestic felicity and accrue goodwill.

"I'm thinking," you say instead, "about how it is you can look so beautiful, even on mornings like this."

Although this is in no way what you were thinking, it is also not entirely untrue. Bethany's brand of beauty is the kind that gets you into nightclubs owned by movie stars and shows through even the worst hangovers—which is not at all important as you both passed the stage in drinking where one suffers hangovers weeks ago. For you and Bethany, being wrecked and recovering from being wrecked has become freakishly normal.

"I wish," Bethany responds, "that you wouldn't say things like that."

"Why not?"

"Because, I don't know." She stares at her burning cigarette. "Because it makes me uncomfortable."

Last night, late, lying in bed, after several very public drunken scenes in various nightclubs from West Hollywood to Marina del Rey, you and Bethany had an intense, honest, private argument, the details of which are just now coming back to you—

filtered through a blood alcohol level you imagine to still be at least .015.

"Oh, well, in that case," you say. Smug, a little mean.

"Jesse," Bethany says, "just stop."

Later, you will drive Bethany to the studio at Universal where she will be late for work as a seamstress in the wardrobe department. You have told your friends back in New York that she's a designer—which is not a total lie because she did work as one for two weeks in June when the real one came down with an especially nasty case of stomach flu. You are finishing your masters at UCLA film school and have a summer job you don't enjoy, can't seem to get to very often and will soon, with any luck, lose.

"You're going to be late for work," you say.

"It won't be the first time," Bethany says.

This kind of understatement is characteristic of Bethany's brand of banter. The first night the two of you went out ended at 11 a.m. the next day with your getting a parking ticket and Bethany being four hours late for work. You are aware, however, that you are not the only person of the male gender responsible for Bethany's bout with excessive tardiness.

"It's not so much going to work that bothers me," Bethany smiles. "It's that they expect me to stay. I mean, I like the drive and all." Bethany enunciates each word not unlike a five-year-old child, seemingly uncertain exactly of how the words will sound and mildly surprised that they all come out in the right order. You are immeasurably charmed by this. You do realize, however, that this seeming ad lib is a piece of well-rehearsed cocktail party conversation.

Bethany doesn't drive to work. She rides a bicycle, and furthermore it's mostly uphill and she hates it.

You should let this go. In the social contract the two of you have established, remarks such as this one are not only acceptable, but expected. Your inability to continue the maintenance of that social contract, you remember, moved from the wings to center stage in last night's argument.

"That was some night," you say, fully aware that every night has been more or less "some night" since you were introduced to Bethany by one of her college roommates. Or, more accurately, since you were warned about Bethany by one of her college roommates.

"Yes," Bethany says. She pours herself more coffee and lights another cigarette from the stove.

"Beth," you say, "I'm crazy about you." You had not planned to say this. You might as well go for broke. "And I know you're crazy about me."

"I see," she says, mashing out her cigarette.

"Faulkner once wrote," you say, "that between grief and nothing—I would choose grief." You turn away to look out the window. "But I am not William Faulkner."

"Jesse," Bethany says, her voice full of the slow, exaggerated caution one uses when one may, quite possibly, be speaking with a lunatic. "What the hell are you talking about?"

"I'm talking about us, Beth. I can't do this anymore. Every night for us is like a New Year's Eve party full of psychopaths. I mean, every night is like shaking dice." You know that you are being spectacularly unpersuasive. You also realize that you are making almost no sense. You consider telling Bethany that together you could be the next Scott and Zelda. Then you remember what happened to Zelda. You decide this is not a good tack. You also remember what happened to Scott, but this is not something you can afford to think about right now.

"I need more from you," you say. "I need commitment."

"Um," Beth says. "Um," she says again.

"I mean…"

You stop talking. You realize you have nothing more to say. In tennis parlance, the ball is no longer in your court. You realize, upon understanding this, the ball hasn't been in your court for quite some time. This is the argument you had last night. This is the argument you have been having since you met. This, you also realize, for the first time, is the last time you can have this argument.

You will understand, a few days later—in the middle of a lecture on *Contempt*— that things must get as ugly and as vicious as they are about to. Only then, with your backside half-asleep pinned to the auditorium's stunningly uncomfortable seat and your eyes pegged to a chiaroscuroed still of Brigitte Bardot's frozen, perfect grimace, will you comprehend that the only way you can keep yourself away from Bethany is to make perfectly and unquestionably sure that she will never want to see you again.

WILL TAKE PAYPAL

EBAY- Item # 343390804238

23 Year Friendship with Don W. copyeditor/playwright manqué

BUY IT NOW: $3,700 *or* will trade for used boat in good condition

DESCRIPTION OF ITEM: Struck up mid-scramble from an anti-war protest on the outskirts of a tony Philadelphia college after the arrival of tear gas wielding police, this high-utility, long-term friendship has been painstakingly assembled, bonding experience by bonding experience. Developed initially through numerous late night coffee-fueled dissections of Clash lyrics and bandying about the names of poorly comprehended existentialist philosophers, friendship at auction eventually assumed the characteristics of adult amity through a series of traded favors, beginning with Don W.'s uncomplaining assistance loading seller's admittedly unwieldy collection of vintage Royal typewriters onto a 14-foot U-Haul in his move to Providence, Rhode Island, for graduate school. Seller, in turn, provided nearly innumerable beer-soaked hours of long distance consolation following Don

W.'s college sweetheart, Kelly Pierce, slipping off to Tucson to marry that asshole, Ray Cameron, CPA.

Even separated by hundreds of miles, a surfeit of meaningful interactions—the kind that instill a profound and unique sense of connectedness—deepened the friendship presently on the auction block. We're talking thousands of dollars of mid-day long distance (before flat fee service) complaining about the sad banality of jam bands, the callous, unworkable agenda of the GOP and the Pittsburgh Pirates staggering inability to maintain quality pitching rotation. These indissoluble bonds of friendship were further cemented through a series of increasingly exotic guy-cations including: fly fishing trips to remote western locales to indulge in fireside evenings rife with male bonding over the filleting of trout; domestic ski trips to progressively more challenging venues (a snapped fibula leading to a near threesome with ginger orthopedist in Telluride, Colorado); culminating in a summer getaway to the Czech Republic, albeit long after the majority of tall, ash blond Czech girls had tired of know-it-all Americans butchering their beautiful language and swilling their beer.

Not sold yet? Don W.'s (thoughtful, soft-spoken late night addresses detailing society's overarching—if well-hidden—need for art that restores our collective faith in the human spirit function as a perfect anodyne for any working writer, visual artist, musician or composer at the end of a largely thankless day. Furthermore, because they represent the sum total of Don W.'s own creative work as he is perpetually overwhelmed by copy editing hundreds of pages of securities brochures in the belly of large investment bank while still claiming to be a playwright) one can rest assured your newly-purchased friendship will never be immolated by all-consuming envy after he succeeds wildly beyond what you consider the merits of his talent—as may have happened to some of your other long-standing colleagues. Here's looking at you, Paul in Missoula!

Lest the friendship at auction seem too limited to yield the close companionship you're looking for, please note that ties have been renewed following seller's return east to accept a Visiting Assistant Lecturer position at the Delaware Valley Community College for Troubled Teens. Ongoing activities include: drinking binges at Lou's Café followed by the occasional action movie or bitchfest lamenting the tragically unfulfilled potential of the Obama presidency and/or the unfortunate lack of imagination presently ruining the American Movie Classics' series *The Walking Dead*.

Full disclosure: several recent, perhaps less successful, interactions could bear some responsibility for this friendship's very reasonable BUY IT NOW price. These activities possibly involved seller's shitfaced attendance at a kindergarten holiday choral recital as a prelude to steeping Don W. in capital T trouble with his uptight, new, and religious wife by supplying an eighth ounce of high-quality cocaine and two inebriated, leggy Hooters waitresses in a sincere, if misguided, attempt to enliven an impromptu Christmas Eve pub crawl several foggy weeks back.

Thanks and Happy Bidding!

Seller's Other Auctions Include:

Brunch with Seller's Dad. Over steaming platters of high-sodium breakfast food at the Valley Diner, seller's Marine Corps retiree father will unreservedly lambaste your non-existent retirement fund, bemoan your character precluding the possibility of a career in the armed forces and grouse about the embarrassingly low pay of academics in the humanities—all as a prelude to his shopworn inquiry as to why you did not attend law school (you were accepted to Georgetown!)—after which he will cut his eyes toward the window, stare at the skeletal deciduous trees and scowl grimly, before *really* laying into you for the utter profligacy of your desire to own—on your head-shakingly meager salary—a boat in good, bad, or any other condition.

NAME THAT YOUTH

Antoinette.
Brenda.
Calandra.
Please, nothing from *Star Trek*.

Carmelita.
Clothilde.
What is *wrong* with you?
You just don't like Clothilde
No one would like Clothilde. Cossette.
Oy.

Dominique.
Delfina.
Dolores.
Okay, Dominique.
I've changed my mind. (Asshole!)

Emma.
Elena.
Ermengarde.

Just, no.

Francis.
Fairfax.
Like Connecticut?
Uh. Yeah...okay. Forget it.
Felicia
Fatima.
F-a-t-ima? Ever *been* to an elementary school?

Giselle.
Model.
Gretel.
Fairytale.
Ganymede.
Just stop.

Hannah.
Havana.
Heloise.
That's silly.
You liked Havana.

Honoria.
You are *such* a jerk.

Jemima.
Jesus, let's just name her Bong-hittia.

Jasmine. Ex-girlfriend.
Lavinia. God, no.

Meredith, then.
I have a niece named that.
Christ. Marilyn.

Really?
No. Not really.

Is there anything that means "Daughter of a Maniac."
Man-eye-i-ca.
She'll never spell that.

Marcie.
Millicent
Too modern. Mackensie.
One word: Phillips.
Oh. Damn.

Melpomene.
You're mispronouncing that.
....Shit. You're right. Mercy.
Meridian.

Nell.
Nikoletta.
Don't even think about it. I remember that bitch.
Novelle.
Short list?
Nah.

Octavia.
I can't even stand the way you *say* that.

Penelope.
I hate your Mom's name.
Since when?
Since now. Pamela.
Pia.
El-e-*ment*-ary school. Can you *hear* me?
Perdita.

What? Afraid 'Piehole' was taken?

Quinn.
VJ.
God. We're *old*.

Rhiannon.
Kidding, right.
Kidding. Rosalind.
Like Russell?
Like Russell.
She *was* cool.
Riley. Ripley. Rubicon.
Don't push your luck.

Simone.
Too French. Sasha.
Sandy.
Too household pet.

Tara.
Terra.
Tatiana.
Ex-girlfriend's cat.
So we're excluding *other* people's pets now?

Verity.
No.
C'mon. Verity. It's a great name.
I hate it.
That's because you suck.

What about Vladimira?
Are you high?

She can go by Mira.
Where the hell would she go?

Violetta. Valeria. Vallerie.
V is an adversarial letter. Valentina, then.

We're running out of letters.
We're running out of letters.

SHE, CLAUDIA

ONCE UPON A TIME....WELL, doubtfully just once, and in all likelihood across a broad array of cultures throughout different periods of history, if you're interested in the narratological point of view (which I suspect, peruser of this literary artifact, you may be) **there was a girl,** which is, from a feminist perspective, well worth considering why so many of these cautionary tales offer—now I've let the cat out of the bag or the linear out of the narrative or at the very least unintentionally provided some kind of authorial hint as to the kind of story being told about **a compact blond girl from Reseda with tits like cantaloupes and a neediness devouring as any black hole in blackest outer space** which represents every... Christ, there I go again... Note to self: The teller of the tale is *not* the interpreter of the tale. Note to reader: You will have to decide just what exactly, if anything, she represents. Please refrain from construing the above as a blanket endorsement of reader response criticism, reception theory, or phenomenology. Certainly not phenomenology!

So, as it stands— if we can conceive of a narrative as standing, then why not sitting, slouching, drawing to an inside straight or for that matter yet again losing every last nickel of another goddamn mortgage payment stupidly betting trifectas at Santa Anita? —we have **a slender, clever, sad, untethered protagonist**—from the Greek agon or contestant—**who minces, sidles, struts, stomps, parades and preens down Ventura Boulevard from Coldwater to Colfax under the sad sway of a dozen desiccated date palms approaching the end of their 50-year life span, which may easily exceed the lifespan of the compact blond girl** at least if the author continues to impel her heedlessly into men's cars to perform what some (granted, probably not *this* author or *this* audience) might describe as unspeakable acts, raising, of course several questions: first among equals, why the author feels compelled to create a compact blond girl only to place her in such mundane jeopardy and further, why the insatiable appetite for narrative centered on characters navigating garish circumstances (17 fucking seasons of *SVU!?*) dominates, often pushing audiences to spend their time ensnared in the exploits of young women who, like this one, **exposes the curved bottoms of her tight butt cheeks as she leans into a late model Cadillac asking the industry-standard question, "Want a date?"**

The penumbra of sodium vapor buzzing above this debauched tableau, the same sodium vapor lights that for dozens of nights haunted and compelled the narrator— who is not to be confused with the author, as the former exists as a vehicle of conveyance for the story, while the latter directs the action from the shadows. Of course, backstage the psyche of the author is manipulated by large-scale cultural and socio-economic forces seen, if at all, through a page darkly, while he is likely also struggling with deep feelings of worthlessness that he attempts to overcome by entertaining—that is to say, confusing attention with love, as the compact blond girl perhaps confuses taking money to open her legs with being valued as she catches a glimpse of her desirable self reflected in a badly lit Ventura Boulevard storefront whose lights **chiaroscuro her high,**

thin cheekbones as she climbs into the front seat of the Cadillac.

She, Claudia, summons the confidence and glare-eyed bravado requisite to perform the task at hand, which is to be used by the overweight man with the fading navy tattoo and flat front trousers, balding, smelling like garlic and brake fluid and of course also to be used by the narrator, the author, and you dear reader—we're all hard at work for the moment using Claudia for our own purposes.

The man, we'll forego assigning a name that either, weighted by literary allusion, may direct us like a one way sign in a unintentional direction or by its very genericness push us to view this bulge-gutted lout as some sort of morally down-at-the-heel Everyman speeding out across the San Fernando Valley, palms damp on the wheel, fingers tapping along with Tony Bennett, making small talk, turning the air conditioning up, prepares himself for what's to come by holding in his mind's eye the sand colored legs of his ex-wife's younger sister on a tangerine king-size bedspread in a Ramada Inn in Sheep Springs, New Mexico during a shared vacation ten months back, a woman with whom he had often imagined himself having sex, the confession of which—to his wife at a table too near the kitchen in an Albuquerque Waffle House—later that week will be the straw that snaps him right into divorce court.

Discussing the costs—only in terms of American currency—of various sexual acts, the man drops his meaty hand heavy onto the blond girl's left thigh, lets his fingers drift up to the hem of her boy shorts the kind that the author certainly didn't wear working as a prostitute in West Hollywood after matriculating from one of California's more prestigious writing programs where he drafted writing four well-optioned (but unproduced) screenplays in a claustrophobic office on Little Santa Monica Boulevard— as the directness of the correlation would be too clumsy, too artless, but instead researched the underpants in question using the techy, free WiFI connection provided by the empty, elegant Hollywood bar in which he's trying to get all this down**, a powder blue pair of size eights that bunch around the thighs she spent the morning trimming, with a jog around the Hollywood Reservoir after waking up early at a regular's post and beam on Arrowhead Drive. The blond girl, our Claudia, is pleased in a complicated, self-destructive way that she's as comfortable reclined on the pilling cloth seats of the fat man's aging CTS rumbling past the sad, low slung houses of Van Nuys as she was sprawled on the off-white Barcelona chair in the great room of a drafty architectural with its full-on views of the glittering microchip of the San Fernando Valley, as she is checking into bungalow Number 3 with her writer husband—that is to say, not comfortable at all.**

While the cliché "the whore with the heart of gold" leaves her cold as the slow-melting ice in my bourbon as I attempt to be quiet enough for story Claudia to tell me which way her tale is moving, as I wait for real Claudia to return from her "date" in the valley and meet me here at Bar Marmont on Sunset Boulevard, where we'll drink shots of Patrón Añejo and she'll complain briefly and with a sense of resignation about what happened at Santa Anita before giving me the rundown on another hotel blow job (she spat; he was used to it) as she lives out **the cliché of being too good for this world— that motivates her** nearly as much as the cliché of the writer being simultaneously raised up and dissipated by Hollywood motivates the author, leading them both into dubious exploits where risks quite obviously outweigh rewards and have impelled Claudia **to marry a writer who's just fine with letting —even encouraging— her to destroy herself every California night in small ways just to ensure her returning with the close-to-the-bone energy necessary to crafting stories sought out by a public he sees (perhaps accurately, perhaps less so) as wanting nothing so much as sensationalism—as tales of his own acrobatics on society's raggedy edges have already been bled out in a broad array of other literary artifacts.**

WORSHIP, KINSHIP, IMITATION, FLATTERY

THREE-QUARTERS THROUGH A HANDLE of Early Times, my wife and I celebrate the memory of noted American author Raymond Carver. I call nine-year-old Eric, "her mouthy teenage son." She heaves my shoes across the yard. An ashtray sails through the stormdoor of the rental house. She makes peanut butter and jelly sandwiches instead of ham. I throw them on the kitchen floor. She kicks the dog and sulks against the chimney, staining a blouse.

We search all the winter coats for loose change. Drop Eric at her mother's. Sneak a pint of Teacher's into Jim's Bar to keep things going through Happy Hour. A couple joins us in a booth. Another. Everyone talks about love. Consumed with envy, we rush home to fuck. Instead, I drink the champagne she's been saving for New Year's Eve, claiming imminent refrigerator failure. She chops up my art supplies with a wood maul, tells me she's been fucking her supervisor. I punch her face till bones snap, feed the last of her vitamins to Vietnam Veterans who keep saying, "pussy." She suggests I move out. I tell her to buck up. "Tomorrow it's Cheever."

A SMALL, IMPORTANT MOMENT AT THE CORNER OF HOLLYWOOD AND FAIRFAX

THE GIRL BEING LED across the street by her boyfriend works at the Whole Foods on Sunset behind the deli counter. She's maybe five foot one. In heels. Although I doubt she's ever worn heels. One hundred and eighty pounds, maybe one ninety, she's slow. Developmentally delayed. Hell, whatever you want to call it. But she's nice. Friendly.

In the supermarket, I always make a point of saying hello and asking how her day is going. Invariably, I stop by to chat, make small talk, what have you—even when I need nothing from the deli.

Last night I saw her with the boyfriend at the video store on Las Palmas. The boyfriend too seemed a few reels short of a feature. They rented *Lady and the Tramp* and a couple of horror movies—some damn Robert Englund crap.

Anyway, the point of the story, the *reason* I'm telling you this: Today, they're crossing Hollywood Boulevard, which is wide, and has a hell of a lot of traffic. But the light is red. So obviously all the traffic is stopped. It's not going anywhere.

But this guy, her boyfriend, this fucking *retard* is standing in the middle of Hollywood Boulevard holding his hand up, palm out, straight at my Mercedes like a white-glove traffic cop while his girl crosses the street. I have no doubt that if it came to it, he would throw himself in front of a goddamn bus before it struck this girl.

Less than twenty seconds later, I am in the middle of a powerful crying jag. Actually *overwhelmed* by tears—I mean I can't see to drive—I have to pull over on Crescent Heights. My thoughts go like this:

I am the vice president of business affairs at a talent agency that represents people who win Best Actor Oscars. I live in a large 50s modern in Benedict Canyon and drive an S Class Mercedes. And I'm absolutely fucking certain—certain as I've ever been of anything in my life—that the guy trying to stop stopped traffic as his homely, backward girlfriend crossed the Boulevard is a better human being than I can possibly hope to become.

PAPARAZZI BLACK ROCK AT FRANK MARTIN'S NUMBER THREE

NOW

NOT UNLIKE, we imagine, most men committing what looks to be a haphazardly planned armed robbery in broad daylight, the guy holding the .22 pistol looks nervous. He also seems impatient, and more than a little angry as the bartender explains there's next to nothing in the register because it's two o'clock in the fucking afternoon and no one is drinking yet. The robber twitches his shadow of a mustache and shakes the handgun like a maraca at the empty bar room. He wears chinos, a summer oxford, skinny tie—as if he were attending an eighties-themed prom. He has likely dressed up for this robbery, we decide. After two shots go into the ceiling and he flees with only a knock-off watch and three empty wallets, the barman shouts at his back, "Don't give up your day job, asshole."

BEFORE

We're deep in our cups at a dark bar on Mercer Street called Frank Martin's. Hollister has bought the last four rounds unreciprocated—tequila—trying to guilt me into asking open-ended questions about his new job following Ashton Kutcher around Soho for the next week trying to photograph the star in unflattering positions (nose picking and crotch scratching are gold) for an editor with whom we both attended RISD—a slight, arrogant man who now sits at a grubby particle board desk at the *National Enquirer's* Florida offices and last month paid Hollister eight thousand dollars for a picture of Russell Crowe kicking a dog.

Hollister has relished paying for the drinks, flipping a fresh fifty from the straining money clip in his breast pocket onto the freshly-wiped bar. He knows that my having a job period is pretty much week-by-week now, what with the cutbacks and the photo of the panting Weimaraner I sent in place of the snapshot of a topless Sienna Miller I'd promised for last month's Hot Bitches special issue of the *Newark Men's Journal*. Of course Hollister also suspects I'm holding out on him. And, yeah, I fucking well am. Three trips to the bathroom in the last 90 minutes—not one of them to piss and not a word about the eight ball crackling in my pocket. Of course underneath all the bluster, Hollister may not give a Siberian tiger turd about the blow or the Kutcher job, not least because he's smart enough to recognize this sadness for what it is.

Ten years back we saw ourselves tuning the art world on its ear with our ruthless innovation or at worst giving in to the mundane drive toward celebrity. None of us are going to end up Richard Avedon, Hollister is telling me when I demonstrate the sloppy bad form to bring this up. I'm okay with that, he says. I'm making mortgage payments. My kid is kicking ass at Columbia Grammar. I had a nice write-up on the *Art Forum* blog after the café show on Ludlow last month.

I have no cards to play this trick. No marriage, no kids and I'm barely making rent in a Greenpoint share. Nothing sold at my last show. My current girlfriend is twenty-three and I suspect she uses crystal meth. Sipping Hollister's free tequila, I think about the way she talks about going to sex clubs without me and I realize it's been months since I've had a thought that wasn't spun into a bundle of nervous energy tangled around a dark core of regret. Dark core of regret? Are things really so arch? Hollister asks and I realize this is all out loud and long before he can form a question about Tina's traipsing off to Sinsation alone last Thursday I bite the bullet. In a voice that begs nothing but jaded complaint, I say, So, Hollister, Ashton Fucking Kutcher, eh? but the door flaps open before he gets out a word.

LATER

Sculpted from caulking compound liberally spiced with high-grade crystal meth, the ambulance attendants look muscular under their starched whites as they carry a wounded (real! live! wounded!) photographer toward the door. Thousands of elaborately carved wax "blood droplets" inscribed with the Patrón logo dangle from the gurney on ultrafine monofilament line. Bright resin specially-engineered to maintain its viscosity, pours ceaselessly onto the floor simulating a lethal amount of freshly spilled blood. Out of sight a man wearing earmuff style hearing protection fires a .45 caliber pistol into a sandbag every thirty seconds as police sirens wail on unseen speakers. The guts of a Nikon D300 are scattered across the floor in a Cy Twombly of damaged circuitry. A life-size Russell Crowe sculpted from dried, aged beef glowers across the room, a smoking Luger flashing in his outstretched hand in time with the unsimulated gunshots. A Lhasa Apso at his feet nibbles.

Hovering near the free wine, two snarky, low-heeled critics from *Installation Nation* roll their eyes. Hollister, they gripe, that poor guy's really starting to show some wear and tear. After the transfusions at the Tate Modern and the Whitney Biennial, not to mention the spleen transplant following the private show at Leo Castelli, they don't think he's got much left to give. But between the clamoring buyers and the Patrón sponsorship we're making a killing. And we had damn well better be. Because neither spleens, nor press coverage, come cheap.

THE LAST TIME I SAW RICHARD

THE CHRISTIANS HAD DRUG HIM, heels first, from behind the lectern centered by the freethinkers in the café of the Tuscaloosa Barnes & Noble. The booksigning had ended improvisationally with a chair from behind like in pro wrestling and into the narrow walkway beside the dumpster he went, quickly hitched to the chromed rear bumper of a high revving Dodge Ram in the soft Alabama darkness. Chortling and guffawing over the shrill trill of Fox News Radio, the Baptists smirked and sneered. Screeching with one colossal ignorant voice, "God ain't no delusion here, you damn limey ass pirate!" they roared off across the macadam lot for the TGI Fridays as Dawkins came apart slowly with much fanfare and gnashing of teeth.

YOUNG AMERICANS, AUGUST 1979

WHIRLING across the spongy deck behind his parents' singlewide, we slide from one rain-slick 2"x 4" to the next. Tuxedo shirt unbuttoned to my navel, prom gown ripped to accommodate his shoulders, we spin between the dripping rails. Twist. Feather step. Closed change. Freeze. Wrenching a hank of hair, I jerk him forward, force him down with the meat of my palm. On his knees he scores the paleness of my stomach with lipstick traces trailing toward the jock strap swollen with knotted panties. I offer nothing but a performative sneer. My fingers push across his cheekbone smearing pancake makeup into eyeliner. I revel in the chiaroscuro— my dark nails against his platinum wig in the streetlight haze. A mile down the tracks, our three-street town feels far as Mars. The saxophone flourishes echoing into the jack pines hold me like I'm holding him, like I've never been held before. This flashbulb moment is nothing less than transfiguration. We are being reimagined by these key changes, transformed by that snarky baritone. Its haunting melisma charges our molecules as we *chassé* in the drizzle. From here on, things will only get more haphazard, glossy. Our planes never streak into Iowa cornfields. Even our riots will reincarnate as history lessons.

BOYHOOD

WHEN I WAS a young boy growing up in a steel town preoccupied with collapsing in on itself, I wanted to shoot my father with a .22 caliber rifle. He had given me the single shot bolt action rifle for my tenth birthday and for many nights afterward I fantasized about striding into his bedroom in the middle of the night and pushing the barrel flush against his chest as he slept and pulling the trigger.

In these imaginings I would always give some impassioned, self-justifying speech right before squeezing the trigger and seeing the muzzle flash and hearing the crack of the rimfire cartridge propelled down the blued barrel. My father, a former infantryman in the Marine Corps, would have to listen to these speeches because he would be too scared to move. In my pre-assassination screeds I would trumpet my secret strength, extol my individuality and rant about how I wasn't going to take any more of his beatings.

Some mornings after nights like this I would ride in my father's secondhand car down to the unemployment office. My father and his buddies, most of whom were also laid off from the town's steel mills or the bituminous mines, referred to these trips as "going to town."

Once, in the afternoon, as a boy growing up in a steel town pretty far gone irrevocably to shit, I attempted to stab an uncle of mine to death with an eight-inch fish filleting knife. My uncle was a large, bushy-bearded man laid off from his job as a railcar welder. I walked in on him beating my grandmother with a leather belt. She had fallen to her knees in the eat-in kitchen of her frame house. One of her brown hands gripped the Formica corner of the tabletop. She held her other hand above her head, elbow bent at an acute angle to ward off the blows. My uncle's voice filled the room like whiskey and ice cubes can fill a glass. My grandmother's breath was all gasps. Tears streamed from her eyes. She pleaded, "Stop, Eddie. Oh, please, stop."

Oblivious to anything but his own rage, my uncle raised the belt and brought it down again. I watched this happen once, then twice. The third time he brought the belt above his head I picked up the fillet knife from a cutting board next to a brook trout on the sideboard near the door. I ran toward my uncle, cursing him, fillet knife held out in front of me like a sword. My uncle turned. With the back of his hand, he knocked me sprawling. When my father came in from parking the car, he saw the condition my grandmother was in, put my uncle in a wrestling hold, later called the volunteer ambulance service.

What I'm trying to bring home to you is this: even though the biggest part of me feels like these things happened in another lifetime, happened—almost—to someone else, that's never going to be the important part. Day or night, I can be inside out with the need to twist this darkness into some *trompe l'oieil* kind of virtue, into something I can wear like grace.

GDANSK

THIS IS NOT your first time in St. Stanislaus's Cathedral.

The January evening after shoplifting the pregnancy test for Miriam, you were grateful to duck in the side door under the frieze when the *policja* unexpectedly gave chase. Months later, the wet afternoonof her funeral—a complication, "unforeseeable," they said—you sweat in the pew near the font between her weeping college friends arm to arm in their heavy, wool coats and her scowling relations with hands folded like napkins. You rolled your eyes as her Uncle Karel—blind with Serbian plum brandy—hugged the pulpit, mumbling about the lord forgiving all manner of sin. Through the swirl of incense, you felt your kneecaps burn, considered the seamless ocean, the way back home. You weighed the operatic spangling of love against your present inability to draw a breath, against the surety that in shuffling from the ICU to the sad, sleek lobby of Jawna Paula II—flat whine of the monitor in your ears—you had been broken irrecoverably. Eyes locked on the empty cathedra, you knew the only way to survive this pageant was to shake it off like water. But now you're back, counting your breaths in a polished pew. The early afternoon light in the nave is soft, diffused, you imagine, by the leaded clerestory windows. The priests, in all likelihood, are still deeply conservative, full of quiet condemnation. But this is not your country. What do you know, really? In twenty-four months at sea, you have understood nothing. Considered little beyond the ticking need to return to this last place to hold station under the enormous golden chandelier, stare into the blank eyes of the marble statuary lining the transepts, recall the blue metallic shimmer of the casket, the cloying smell of lilies.

THE HIGHWAY SOUND

MY AUNT LOOKS up at the low, gray sky swirling across the interstate, says to hurry our asses back into the convenience store. My brother Freddy (Walkman) and my sister Annette (Sweet Valley High #23) pay no mind—maybe because we've only met her twice before our dad's funeral, maybe because this cross-country drive is bullshit, maybe because we don't want to live in a split level in Bangor, Maine. But Aunt Doris grabs their bony arms like an angry gym teacher, whisks them across the macadam. Already sprawled in the passenger's seat, I watch the sky thicken and drop. The flag above the gas pumps blows straight as a ruler. Pick-ups, trailer trucks, a Harley-Davidson motorcycle all slide off the exit a dozen miles west of Tulsa, Oklahoma.

In the distance, a dark thread of sky teases downward toward the roofline of a midrise hotel. A siren pierces the afternoon. Other kids, other parents hop from their cars, rush for the doors of the Jiffy Trip. Dust devils whip litter through the lot. Tumbleweeds shoot past my aunt's Toyota. Splashes of rain slap its windshield, pop off its sea blue hood. When I shoulder the passenger door open into the wind, there's nothing to smell but ozone. Freddy and Annette huddle with Aunt Doris in the store near the ice cream cooler. Aunt Doris is frantic, scanning the parking lot. When she catches sight of me still messing by the car, she tries to elbow her way through the crowd, but the store is jammed tight with people and she can't really move. I let go of the door of the Corolla. The wind slaps it shut with a bang. I start toward the center of the lot to feel this heavy air brush my body like a hand, to feel it lift me into the sky green as a lawn.

IN ORDER TO LIVE

DURING A LULL, my writing class talks about the upcoming Christmas holidays, the presents, the dinners, the visits home. I describe my discovering Santa Claus wasn't real the Christmas Eve my parents got loaded and made me fetch all the presents from the upstairs hall closet behind the rollaway bed and cart them down the stairs myself, shove them under the Douglas Fir next to the small ceramic nativity set shrouded in slivers of white cellophane.

My teacher whistles a puff of air between his thinning lips. He says, "Man, that's a great story."

I shake my head. Explain how they apologized later, when I was in junior high after they'd each done a couple of turns at Hazelton, got sober.

The teacher ignores me. He goes on about how the story does a great job using symbolism, the way one incident stands in for all the mistakes that fall under the heading of bad parenting. Of course no one would really do that to a kid, he says. But because it's so unthinkingly cruel, because it offers such a stark, stripped down example—a single incident involving a terrible betrayal of an innocent—it says a lot about the horrible mistakes humans make in the process of parenting children, reminds us

how vulnerable our best intentions are. The other kids in exposi-
tory writing decide his "vulnerability of our intentions" bit is
really the nuts and nod, raising their eyebrows.

Not yet tearing up, I tell them it's not a story about parental
failure. My parents had me bring the presents down so my
younger brother and sister wouldn't wake up to find nothing
under the tree on Christmas morning. My parents did it out of
love.

"Lynn," my writing teacher looks at me, asks, "Can you
remember what we said on the first day of class is the reason we
tell stories?"

PREVIOUSLY PUBLISHED

A User's Guide to Bringing My Ex-Girlfriend Shelley to Orgasm, *Pindeldyboz* Ab Initio, *Dos Passos Review*
Accrual, *Gargoyle Magazine*
Another Night With Jim, *McSweeney's Internet Tendency*
AutoDestruct, *elimae*
Bob in the Crosshairs, *Heartwood*
Boyhood, In State and That Highway Sound, *Post Road*
Cleaning House, *New World Writing*
Cleanliness, *StoryGlossia*
Color Scheme, *5_TROPE*
Down Along the Condado, *The Watershed*
Fable of the Deconstruction #473: Jameson on Polish Hill, *Snow Monkey*
Four Hard Facts About Water, *Vestal Review*
Four Ways of Looking at Nashville, *Kudzu*
Gdansk, *New Orleans Review*
He Needs Your Help!, *The Pittsburgh Quarterly Online*
Ice Water, Here on Earth, *Pittsburgh City Paper*
If I Could Only Tell You One Story, *Caketrain*
In Order to Live, *DOGZPLOT*

In the Land Between the Valley and the Hills, What Men Said,
They Meant, *Hobart* Jesus in 42, *failbetter.com*
Kampala 2012, *Contrary Magazine*
Life Lesson, *Smokelong Quarterly*
The Margarita Truce of South Fifth Street, *Pithead Chapel*
Quitting with Jimmy, *New Delta Review*
Scalene, *Right Hand Pointing*
Shooting Elvis, *Worcester Review*
The Food Speakers, *Alimentum*
The Fungible Trajectories of Carol, *Word Riot*
This Is Not a Story About Last Chances, *JMWW*
Worship, Kinship, Imitation, Flattery *Hot Metal Bridge*
Young Americans, August 1979, *Still: The Journal*

ACKNOWLEDGMENTS

There is no shortage of people to thank for helping make this collection possible. Early teachers like Lewis Nordan and Chuck Kinder were instrumental in helping me learn to tell a story in ways readers might find interesting. Beta-readers, John and Don, your friendship, excellent suggestions and patience over the years are legendary. Big thanks to the Blue Mountain Center for their generous support, and to all of the journals and magazines kind enough to publish stories along the way. Thanks too to Leza and Christoph at CLASH for believing in the book. I would also like to convey my gratitude to all the detective agencies that hired me to guard empty buildings between teaching gigs. This collection simply wouldn't exist without all those places I had to be with time to do nothing but write.

Damian Dressick is the author of the novel *40 Patchtown*. His creative work has appeared in more than fifty literary journals and anthologies, including W.W. Norton's *New Micro: Exceptionally Short Fiction*, *Post Road*, *New Orleans Review*, *Cutbank*, failbetter.com, *Hobart*, *Smokelong Quarterly*, and *New World Writing*. A Blue Mountain Residency Fellow, he is the winner of the Harriette Arnow Award and the Jesse Stuart Prize. He co-hosts WANA: LIVE, a virtual reading series that brings some of the best in Appalachian writing to the world. He teaches at Clarion University of Pennsylvania.

For more, check out www.damiandressick.com

ALSO BY CLASH BOOKS

MARGINALIA

Juno Morrow

BORN TO BE PUBLIC

Greg Mania

LIFE OF THE PARTY

Tea Hacic

HEXIS

Charlene Elsby

GIRL LIKE A BOMB

Autumn Christian

I'M FROM NOWHERE

Lindsay Lerman

COMAVILLE

Kevin Bigley

SILVERFISH

Rone Shavers

POINTS OF ATTACK

Mark de Silva

WE PUT THE LIT IN LITERARY

clashbooks.com

FOLLOW US

Twitter

IG

FB

@clashbooks

EMAIL

clashmediabooks@gmail.com

Printed in the USA
CPSIA information can be obtained
at www.ICGtesting.com
JSHW022343140824
68134JS00019B/1662

9 781944 866860